*"Put me dow***   *said*
*breathless***

"No. You a___   ___ut of
your system. ___   ___ you where I
stand," Houst___   ___ arms holding her
snugly.

"If you insist.__

"Look at me, January," he ordered, his voice deep and rumbly.

She did, and felt her body tremble beneath his gaze. Heated desire was pulsing through her, Houston was driving her crazy with want of him—and he knew it! "Please, Houston, tell me," she said softly.

He brushed her lips with his and cradled her against him. "I want you, January St. John," he murmured, nibbling at her lower lip.

"I want you, too, Houston, but—"

"Later," he said, and claimed her mouth in a hard, searing kiss that promised everything she'd been dreaming about since she met him . . .

WHAT ARE *LOVESWEPT* ROMANCES?

They are stories of true romance and touching emotion. We believe those two very important ingredients are constants in our highly sensual and very believable stories in the *LOVESWEPT* line. Our goal is to give you, the reader, stories of consistently high quality that may sometimes make you laugh, sometimes make you cry, but are always fresh and creative and contain many delightful surprises within their pages.

Most romance fans read an enormous number of books. Those they truly love, they keep. Others may be traded with friends and soon forgotten. We hope that each *LOVESWEPT* romance will be a treasure—a "keeper." We will always try to publish

LOVE STORIES YOU'LL NEVER FORGET
BY AUTHORS YOU'LL ALWAYS REMEMBER

The Editors

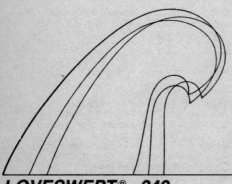

LOVESWEPT® • 249

Joan Elliott Pickart
January in July

BANTAM BOOKS
TORONTO • NEW YORK • LONDON • SYDNEY • AUCKLAND

JANUARY IN JULY

A Bantam Book / April 1988

LOVESWEPT® and the wave device are registered
trademarks of Bantam Books. Registered in U.S. Patent
and Trademark Office and elsewhere.

All rights reserved.
Copyright © 1988 by Joan Elliott Pickart.
Cover art copyright © 1988 by Nick Caruso.
No part of this book may be reproduced or transmitted
in any form or by any means, electronic or mechanical,
including photocopying, recording, or by any information
storage and retrieval system, without permission in
writing from the publisher.
For information address: Bantam Books.

If you would be interested in receiving protective vinyl
covers for your Loveswept books, please write to this address
for information:

Loveswept
Bantam Books
P.O. Box 985
Hicksville, NY 11802

ISBN 0-553-21889-1

Published simultaneously in the United States and Canada

Bantam Books are published by Bantam Books, a division
of Bantam Doubleday Dell Publishing Group, Inc. Its trademark, consisting of the words "Bantam Books" and the
portrayal of a rooster, is Registered in U.S. Patent and
Trademark Office and in other countries. Marca Registrada.
Bantam Books, 666 Fifth Avenue, New York, New York 10103.

PRINTED IN THE UNITED STATES OF AMERICA

O   0 9 8 7 6 5 4 3 2 1

*For my mother, Olive Elliott,
who taught me how to be
a January*

One

June 30

Houston Tyler entered his apartment and slammed the door behind him. He tossed his suit coat onto a chair, pulled off his tie, then unbuttoned his shirt and yanked it free of his pants. During the entire process he scowled.

Houston Tyler was *not* in a terrific mood.

He slouched onto a chair, laced his fingers over his bare chest, and leaned his head back so he could glare at the ceiling. Shifting his massive body, he decided he hated the chair. There had not yet been a chair produced that was comfortable for someone who was six-feet-five and weighed two hundred and thirty pounds. The chair manufacturers of the world had a conspiracy going against big men.

"That's right," he said decisively. Lord, he had an ugly ceiling. Why hadn't he ever noticed before?

He sighed. What else, he wondered, could he gripe

about to postpone thinking about what really had him thoroughly depressed? No, he'd better face it head-on, then figure out what he was going to do to fix it.

He did not look like a man who had just come from a festive, happy occasion, he knew. The wedding of his sister, Austin, and Sam Carter had been great. The ceremony had been held in a judge's chambers, and was followed by a huge reception at a fancy hotel where champagne had flowed, the band had played, and a good time was had by all.

Except Houston.

Oh, he was pleased for his sister and Sam, he mused. They were fantastic together, top-notch, and so in love that they couldn't take their eyes off each other.

And therein was the source of Houston's gloom.

"Well, hell," he muttered. Enough was enough, for crying out loud. In April his parents had celebrated their thirty-fifth wedding anniversary with the glow of love-struck teenagers. Then in May his twin brother, Dallas, had married Joyce and moved to Arizona. Dallas, the crumb, had even gotten a neat five-year-old son in the deal in the form of Joyce's boy, Willie. Now, in June, Austin had just married Sam.

Houston sat up straighter in the chair and glanced at his watch. In fifteen minutes, he realized, it would be a new day, *and* a new month. July. And, by damn, July was his! *He* was going to discover the woman of his dreams. *He* was going to be married. *He* was going to find his partner for life. Nothing would stop him.

Except one niggling obstacle.

Houston leaned forward and rested his elbows on his knees. His frown deepened as he absently ran his finger over the bridge of his nose. There she was, he fumed, front row center in his mind . . . again.

January St. John.

It had been almost two months since he'd met her for the first and only time. Almost two months since that beautiful . . . *bee-yoo-tee-ful* . . . bundle of energy had pulled back her arm, doubled up her fist, and broken his nose!

Lord above, she was something.

He'd gone to Upstate New York from Chicago with his father to see the director of the institute where Austin had stayed years before. Their father had thought it was the perfect place: his daughter, the genius, would be happy, fit in, be accepted for her superior intelligence. But the institute had been all wrong for Austin. Houston had seen that on a surprise visit and hauled his sister out and home.

Since then, the director periodically contacted Austin, causing her great upset. They wanted her to come back, use her mental capabilities to the fullest. Houston and his father, Teddy, had gone to the place to make it clear once and for all that Austin was not to be approached again.

And there she had been—January St. John.

The director had been conducting a tour for a group of wealthy people with the hope of convincing them to donate money to the institute. January had been among those potential benefactors. When the director had seen Houston, recalled how the big man had carried Austin right out of the place, the guy was livid, and all hell broke loose.

Houston chuckled, recalling January's fury when she'd seen the four huge security guards descending on Houston and Teddy. She'd marched right into the middle of the brawl with every intention of decking one of the guards. Houston had seen her coming, was instantly concerned for her safety, and stepped in front of her at the exact moment she swung her little fist.

And she'd broken his nose!

Houston tested the bridge of his nose. He'd never received the proper sympathy from his family for his injury, he thought. They'd laughed themselves silly over the fact that big Houston Tyler had had his nose busted by a pint-size woman. But, damn, his nose had hurt. A lot. For a long time. And nobody cared. Rotten people.

Yep, he thought, sinking back in the chair, January St. John was something. She'd bailed Houston and his father out of jail, got the charges against them dropped, then taken them to the airport in her chauffeured limousine.

And that had been that.

A brief, wild encounter.

Short, and not so sweet, due to his nose.

A chance meeting with a beautiful woman.

In, then out. Hello, then good-bye.

But, Houston thought, narrowing his eyes, it hadn't gone quite that simply. January St. John had crept into his dreams on a nightly basis, inched into his mind during the day, hovered around in his brain like a pesty fly.

He could see her, he realized, as clearly as if she were standing in that very room. She was fairly tall, maybe five-feet-seven, though she didn't seem very big next to him. She had full breasts, soft curves, and nonstop legs. Her hair was short, dark, a tumble of silky curls that framed her face. A face that was incredibly beautiful, with delicate features: a pert nose, lips that looked very kissable, and enormous gray eyes surrounded by long, dark lashes.

January St. John.

And she was driving Houston Tyler out of his ever-lovin' mind!

Why? he continually asked himself. Why couldn't he get that woman out of his mind? She was ruining his life. The women listed in his little black book paled in comparison to January.

January St. John, Houston knew, was so out of his reach, it was ridiculous. She lived in another state; she was old money and big power. She was no older, he was sure, than his soon-to-be twenty-eight, but she had sophistication, class, moved in high-society circles. Houston was blue-collar construction, smart but not brilliant, earned his living with his hands and by the strength of his muscled body. He was separated from January by more than just miles. They were worlds apart in everything, from social standing to the balances in their checkbooks. He knew it and accepted it.

Then why couldn't he forget her?

He looked at his watch. "Ah-ha," he said. "It's July. It is now July, Houston Tyler's month to meet, fall in love with, and marry . . . *the* woman." He would not be stopped. He was sick to death of being alone, of seeing everyone around him marching off in pairs as though heading for Noah's Ark. He wanted a wife and he wanted a baby. A baby created by him and that special someone he was going to find.

And none of it, he thought glumly, was going to happen if he didn't do something drastic about January St. John. She had taken up residence in his brain, and he was going to evict her. Shuffle her off to Buffalo. He hadn't succeeded in two months by mentally yelling at her to leave him alone. So . . . he'd just have to see her in person one more time.

It was the only solution, Houston decided. He needed to actually see her, realize she was beautiful—but so were plenty of others—reaffirm in his mind that she was out of his world and out of his league. He'd free himself of the strange hold she had on him, then proceed with his personal mission of finding a wife. Good plan. Excellent, in fact. Austin wasn't the only genius in the Tyler clan.

Houston slapped his hands onto his thighs, pushed himself to his feet, and smiled. He was between jobs as a construction worker, had some money in his savings; the timing was perfect. He would devote the first part of *his* July to clearing the decks of one January St. John, then get on with his life. Fantastic.

Houston headed for the kitchen for a glass of milk, absently stroking the bridge of his nose as he went.

July 1

January St. John doodled on the pad of paper in front of her, not really hearing the report being given by the man speaking. There were a dozen people seated around the gleaming mahogany table in the boardroom of St. John Enterprises. At the far end of the table opposite January was her mother, Sara St.

John, widow of James, and, for the past five years since his death, the president of the huge corporation.

January had given her report, as she always did on the first day of the month. She was the executive vice-president of the St. John Enterprises foundation, responsible for annual grants in the millions. It was a rewarding, challenging career that she thoroughly enjoyed. She often told her mother that if it weren't for the loss of her father to a sudden heart attack, January would have a perfect existence, a full and exciting life.

Or so she had thought. Lately, January mused, it seemed she'd been plagued by a sense of restlessness, of there being something indefinable missing from her busy life. For almost two months now she'd felt as though she were searching for an unknown entity that wouldn't come into clear focus in her mind. And it was driving her nuts!

January shifted in her chair, slipped her shoes off, then ran her fingertip absently over the knuckles of her right hand. She tried to concentrate on the words being spoken, decided she didn't care diddly if the six magazines they owned were dominating their markets, and went back to her doodling.

Her eyes widened as she stared down at the pad in front of her. It was covered in a variety of printing, writing, and calligraphy, all saying the same thing: Houston Tyler.

Darn that man, January fumed. There he was again. She'd sat there like a space case, writing his name over and over, not even realizing she was doing it. It made no sense whatsoever that a man she had seen only once had the ability to pop into her mind at the most unexpected moments, as well as pop into her dreams at night on a regular basis.

Of course, she reasoned, their meeting, though brief, had hardly been run-of-the-mill. She'd broken Houston's nose, for heaven's sake. Her hand had throbbed for days following the fiasco at the institute—which had *not* been the recipient of any St. John Enterprises money.

Houston. Great, big, beautiful Houston. Lord, he was gorgeous, she thought. He had dark, thick auburn hair, calling to a woman to sink her fingers into it. He was tall and wide-shouldered, had muscles on his muscles, but moved with the easy gait of a man comfortable about his body. Deeply tanned, his features were rugged, as though chiseled from stone, then bronzed by the sun. His voice was a rich rumble, befitting his size.

He was a construction worker, he'd said, and more than once January had found herself imagining him stripped to the waist as he worked, muscles bunching and moving, sweat glistening on his tanned back. And more than once, a curl of heated desire had settled deep, deep within her from the image in her mind.

January shifted in her chair again, then sat still as she glanced at her mother, who was cocking a questioning eyebrow at her. January smiled weakly, then directed her attention to the man who was still droning on.

January wrote Houston's name on the pad of paper again, then flipped it over in self-disgust. Her preoccupation with Houston was absurd. He wasn't remotely like the up-and-coming young executives she dated, the yuppies of Manhattan. They were

Harvard, Yale, Stanford. Houston was blue-collar, sweat, and grime. And muscles. And a beautiful body, yummy hair, lips made for kissing, and— Oh, stop, she told herself firmly.

January tapped the eraser of her pencil against her chin and stared into space. Question: Which had come first, meeting Houston Tyler, then the strange sense of restlessness; or had the restlessness been a bud about to bloom at the time she'd met Houston, causing him to fill a strange void there before his arrival? Interesting question, she decided.

Did the answer matter? she asked herself. No, probably not. Her having met Houston was a chance encounter, and she'd never see him again. He was back in Chicago building whatever it was that he built. She hoped his nose had healed all right. She'd done some fancy verbal footwork during the drive to the airport, asking him if his wife would know how to tend to a broken nose. He wasn't married, he'd said, then she'd volunteered the fact that it was a good thing she wasn't, either, as she'd have no idea what to do for a husband's broken nose.

Oh, so clever. And oh, so dumb, because she'd never see Houston again. And besides, she went on mentally, if he was a construction worker right across the street in Manhattan, it wouldn't change the facts. She and Houston came from different worlds. They wouldn't have a thing in common, nothing going for them at all. Except, of course, that she was a woman and he was a man. Brother, was he ever one hunk of a man!

January sighed, realized that three people around

the table had looked at her and quickly cleared her throat.

"Thank you, one and all," Sara St. John said, recalling January to the situation at hand. "Excellent meeting and, needless to say, I'm delighted with your reports of rising profits. I'll see all of you here next month. January, would you spare me a moment, please?"

Uh-oh, January thought. Time to pay the piper for her less than attentive state of mind during the meeting.

She stood, remembered she wasn't wearing her shoes, and sat back down to wiggle into the soft leather pumps. The other members of the board of directors filed out, and the room became ominously quiet. January stood again, gathered her papers, and walked toward her mother.

Sara St. John was a slim, attractive woman in her fifties with short, curly gray hair and gray eyes that her daughter had inherited. Though she had taken no active role in St. John Enterprises while her husband was alive, he had shared everything with her at the end of his long workdays throughout their long married life. Upon his death Sara had gathered her knowledge, strength, and courage and announced that she was taking over James's place as president. Those who had refused to work constructively with her were wished every success as they exited.

The first year had been a struggle as Sara learned the intricacies of running a conglomerate. January, fresh out of college, stood at her side, as did the staff that had remained loyal to Sara. She hired men and women with new ideas and bubbling enthusiasm to fill the vacancies created by those who had left. Together, as a team, they had flourished. Sara proved to be a shrewd, fair, and honest leader, and profits had grown steadily over the past five years.

But it was Sara, the mother, who now watched her lovely daughter approach, then sit in the chair next to her.

"You," Sara said, smiling warmly, "were a naughty girl."

January sighed. "I know, and I apologize. Paul Dennis is so boring. Did you ever notice that he says 'in conclusion' six times before he actually shuts up and concludes?" She stroked her fingertip over her knuckles.

"Is your hand still bothering you?"

"What?" January jerked her finger back. "No, it's fine."

"That's good," Sara said, still smiling as she glanced at January's hand again, then back to her face.

"That's your smug mother smile," January said, frowning. "The one you use when I feel like you're peering into my brain."

Sara laughed but then grew serious. "January, there is obviously something bothering you. Your work has been excellent, as always, but I sense . . . oh, I don't know. Why don't you tell me what's troubling you?"

January sat back in the chair. "I can't explain it, because I'm not sure what it is. For the last couple of months I've felt . . ." Her voice trailed off.

"Restless?" her mother prompted.

"Yes," January said, looking at her in surprise.

"Restless, edgy, not quite satisfied with your life, wondering what might be missing?"

"See? I told you. You're peeking into my brain."

" 'Tis true. Loving mothers seem to know how to do that. You've been like this ever since you made that trip to the institute. Oh, that was a marvelous adventure. Your father would have adored it." Sara reached for January's pad of paper and looked at it. "Ah, just as I suspected. It all makes sense now. The source of your unrest is Houston Tyler, broken nose and all."

"Well, I—no," January said, squirming in her chair. "Don't be silly. I mean, granted he's beautiful, and big and gorgeous, and has the most magnificent voice. His hair is—but so what? I'll never see him again. And besides, he's a construction worker. Our lifestyles are totally different."

"January St. John, I'll hear none of that," Sara said. "Your father was a millionaire when he stopped along the highway for a cup of coffee. I was a waitress in that greasy-spoon café. You were raised to judge people as people, not measure their worth by their wealth or social standing. Don't use the St. John name and money as an excuse to mask your own fears."

"What fears? I'm not afraid of anything."

"Aren't you? Oh, January, there are so many fine young men flocking after you, and you keep them all at arm's length. Don't you hold them off because of a whisper of fear that they might be seeking you out for what you could do for their careers? You are a St. John. There's no escaping that fact."

"I guess you're right," January said slowly.

"And now, Houston Tyler, construction worker," Sara went on. "A man you met in an exciting moment and can't forget. Worlds apart? I think not. He's constantly on your mind, not a world away."

"You know what I mean. Besides, there's the question."

"What question?"

"The question is," January said, poking a finger in the air, "which came first—Houston or the restlessness, the sense of something missing? It could very well be that I mentally plopped him into a void within me because it was there, and so was he. Or I was fine, met Houston, and because of him, actually because of him, all this turmoil started within me. That, my darling mother, is the question."

"Bravo," Sara said, smiling. "Using your father's analytical bent. You have it sorted out to being either answer A or answer B. Well done."

"Whoop-dee-do," January said sullenly. "It's not well done if I can't get the answer. All I can do is mope, pout, and be miserable."

"Shame on you. St. Johns do not mope and pout. We may yell and throw things on occasion, but we don't pout. You want the answer to your question? Then, my love, go find it."

January blinked. "You're kidding."

"I certainly am not. You have vacation time coming." She smiled. "Besides, you have an 'in' with the president of this outfit. Take all the time you need."

"To do what? Mother, for heaven's sake, I can't march up to Houston Tyler and say I need to spend some time with him so that I can get my head straightened out. That's absurd."

"The details I'll leave to you. You'll think of something."

"But what if . . . I mean, what if I discover that

Houston really is the source of my— Oh, mercy," she said, her hands flying to her cheeks.

"Do keep me posted, dear," Sara said calmly. She rose to her feet. "I must go. I have a lunch date. Oh, and January?"

"Yes?"

"All of your life people have assumed you were named for the month in which you were born, and we know that isn't true. I chose your name because it represented a beginning, something wonderfully new and exciting, which you were to me. The start of each year holds that magical appeal too. As you set out to find your answer, be a January. Be open and receptive to all that the future holds. And listen to your heart."

"Thank you, Mother. I love you so much."

"And I love you. I wish only for your happiness, and I have faith in you that you'll make the right choices. I'll see you later."

" 'Bye," January said quietly. What an incredible woman, she thought. Her mother certainly had more confidence in her than she had in herself. Be a January. Be open and receptive to all that the future holds. Did that future include Houston Tyler? Lord, she didn't know, and at that point in time she had absolutely no idea how to find out. She needed a plan, no doubt about it.

January sighed, shook her head, and got to her feet. She scooped up her papers and stared at the pad covered in Houston's name.

"Darn you, Houston Tyler," she said to the paper. "You are really complicating my life." Oh, brother, she fumed, walking toward the door, in order to find her answer she had to search for and listen to her own inner voices. And she had to figure out how in the heck to see Houston Tyler. "I'd like to break his nose again," she said as she left the room.

Houston was in a lousy mood again.

During the entire day he'd thought up, then rejected, plan after plan that would enable him to see January St. John. A man couldn't walk up to a woman and ask to spend some time with her so he could get her out of his head and get on with his life. If he did, she'd probably break his nose again! And saying he just happened to be in the neighborhood was no good, considering he lived in Chicago and she was in New York. Cripes.

Houston wandered into his small kitchen, opened the refrigerator, and pulled out a bowl of spaghetti. He heated a huge plateful in the microwave, poured a tall glass of milk, then sat down at the table. He ran his finger over his nose as he stared at a calendar on the wall.

He was wasting precious time, he thought. July was his month, and he had to make every second count. He had to come up with a reasonable excuse for showing up on January's doorstep.

"Like what?" he mumbled, twirling spaghetti around his fork. It was halfway to his mouth when the telephone rang. "Hell."

He strode into the living room and snatched up the receiver.

" 'Lo?"

"Hous— Mr. Tyler?"

"Yeah."

"This . . . this is January St. John."

Houston froze, every muscle in his body tensing. His eyes widened, his mouth dropped open, and there was absolutely no air in his lungs.

Oh, Lord, January thought frantically. He wasn't saying a word. He didn't remember who she was. She should hang up and forget the whole darn thing. No, she'd give him one more chance. Just one more.

"Mr. Tyler? Are you there?"

"Call me—" Houston cleared his throat. "—Call me Houston. What can I do for you, Miss St. John?" His heart was going crazy. It was beating like a bongo drum.

"It's January," she said. Oh, that voice, that voice! That deep, rich, rumbly, sexy voice. She couldn't handle this. Yes, she could. She had to. "I . . . how's your nose?" Brilliant.

"Fine. How's your hand?" he asked. Lord, this was dumb. Had she actually called after nearly two months to ask about his nose? She had such a lovely voice. Really, really lovely.

"My hand is splendid." Splendid? she thought. She had to get her act together. Right now! "Houston, the reason I'm calling . . ." This was the best plan she'd come up with. It wasn't great, but it was all she had. Oh, mercy. ". . . is to inquire as to whether you are free to do a brief"—well, not *too* brief—"consulting job for St. John Enterprises."

"Consulting job?"

"Yes, you see, we recently purchased a small island off the coast of Maine. There's a house on it, a very old house. I'd like your opinion as to whether or not it's worth remodeling, or if it should simply be torn down. You did mention as we were driving to the airport that day that you do this sort of thing."

"Yes, I do, but so do lots of others right there in New York."

Now came the tricky part, January thought. If he bought this story, she'd sell him some swampland. "Of course, there are oodles of construction people here. Oodles. But they're busy."

"All of them?" he said, an incredulous tone to his voice.

January cringed. "The Big Apple is getting bigger and bigger," she said brightly. "I've contacted a dozen places, and they can't spare anyone. Amazing, isn't it?"

It was also a bunch of bull, Houston thought. What in the hell was she up to? "Amazing."

"I thought so too. Anyway, I suddenly remembered you." Suddenly remembered? More like *continually*. "Are you interested? We would, of course, pay all your travel expenses, as well as your consulting fee. Well?"

He couldn't believe this. It was the answer to his prayers, the solution to his problem, being handed to him on a silver platter. She was lying through her teeth about there being no one available to do the job, but he'd sort that over in his mind later.

"Houston?"

"When would you want me there?"

"As soon as possible. When can you come?"

"Tomorrow."

"Really?" January said, her eyes widening.

"I'm between jobs."

"Excellent," she said. Tomorrow! No. No, no. She needed time to have a nervous breakdown and recover. Tomorrow? "I'll send the company plane for

you. A car will pick you up at ten in the morning
and take you to the airport. Will that be convenient?"

Company plane? Car to pick him up? Yeah, he
could handle that. "It'll be fine."

"Good. Well, I'll . . . I'll see you soon."

"Soon."

"Good-bye, Houston," she said softly.

"Good-bye, January," he said, then slowly replaced
the receiver. Really, really lovely voice. Forget that,
he told himself. What in the hell was January St.
John up to? Actually, it didn't matter. *His* mission
was clear, and that was what he'd concentrate on.
See January, spend a little time with her—well, not
too little—get her out of his system once and for all.
Then he would get serious about finding himself a
wife. Fantastic.

Houston spun around, went back into the kitchen,
and ate his spaghetti, not even noticing that it was
cold.

January sat staring at the telephone for a full five
minutes after she'd hung up.

She got to her feet and began to pace across her
large living room, not aware as she usually was of
how deliciously the plush, pale blue carpet curled
around her bare toes.

Houston Tyler had actually believed that ridiculous story? she questioned. Somehow she didn't think
so. He was not a dope. Then why had he agreed to
come? Well, why not? He was between jobs and
didn't have anything better to do. That was rather
insulting. No, it didn't matter why, as long as he
came. She had to find her answer before she blew a

fuse in her brain. As to what she would do with that answer . . . well, she'd worry about that later. First things first. One step at a time. Houston was coming tomorrow.

At midnight January decided she'd made a dreadful mistake. She'd very calmly announced to Houston that a car would pick him up and deliver him to St. John Enterprises' private plane. Had that sounded like she was flaunting the fact that she was wealthy? Yes, it probably did. She hadn't intended to do that. Ordering the jet to zip here and there was as natural to her as breathing. She just picked up the phone and did it.

While it could very well be that Houston Tyler meant absolutely nothing whatsoever to her, she still wouldn't dream of humiliating the man. And if he *did* mean something to her? No, she didn't want to think about that yet. It was just too overwhelming to comprehend at the moment.

The issue at hand, the one keeping her from sleeping, was the fact that she'd provided the plane and car for Houston as blithely as someone ordering a pizza to go. If Houston was angry or defensive because of her actions, he wouldn't be giving her a clear picture of who he was. Darn it, she should have done things differently somehow.

Well, it was too late now. The damage, if any, was done. There he'd sit as the lone occupant of that jet, having plenty of time to examine its lush interior, knowing that no expense had been spared in furnishing it.

Unless . . .

Unless he wasn't the only one making the trip
Suppose *she* was on the plane? If Houston's atten
tion was diverted a bit from the plush aircraft,
might soothe his pride, which she'd surely wounded
Yes, that was the only proper, humane, kind thin
to do. And thoughtful. And nice. Her mother woul
be proud of her. It was also the only way to ge
Houston to relax and just be himself. She amaze
herself at times.

With a decisive nod January wiggled into a com
fortable position on her bed and within moment
was deeply asleep.

July 3

Houston was awake before dawn, his thought
going a hundred miles an hour. What did a perso
wear to travel on a private jet? Did he chat with th
pilot? Tip the guy? No doubt there were rules fo
this highfalutin stuff, but he sure didn't know wha
they were.

And, dammit, he thought in the next instant, h
didn't care. He wasn't there to impress anyone. H
didn't care what January thought of him if she hear
he'd blown the etiquette of private planes. Mayb
there was a book on it in the library. It was too earl
to go to the library. No, he didn't care what Januar
thought. Darn it, he had a genius for a sister, wh
had stuff like this stored in her brain. But wher
was Austin when he needed her? Off on her honey
moon, for Pete's sake. That was really very inconsid
erate of her.

Oh, Lord, he moaned, his mind was mush. H

had to remember that he wasn't trying to impress January St. John, he was attempting to get her out of his thoughts. He'd simply be himself, Houston Tyler, and let the chips fall where they may. He had a mission, a purpose, in making this trip, and it had better go as planned. By the time he winged his way home, he'd be free of the strange, lingering memories of January. Free to find the woman of his dreams.

Houston flipped back the blankets and headed for the shower. He'd wear jeans and a T-shirt, he decided. Well, maybe cords and a knit shirt. Then again, there was always slacks and a dress shirt. And, he supposed, he should take along a sport coat in case the air-conditioning was set too low on the plane. But no tie. Absolutely, positively, no tie. Because he was *not* trying to impress January St. John!

Two

He liked limousines.

Houston stretched his long legs out in front of
him, smiled, and nodded. Now a veteran traveler in
limos—this being his second ride in one—he determined that something had finally been invented to
accommodate a big man.

He glanced at the driver, who was decked out in a
perfectly tailored uniform with a billed cap. Houston
smoothed his own tie, which he'd quickly put on
when he'd peered out the window at the approaching driver. If the driver wore a tie, Houston had
reasoned, it seemed only fitting that the passenger
did too.

He looked, Houston mused, as spiffy as he had for
Austin's wedding: brown slacks, yellow shirt, brown
tie, tan sport coat. Not bad. Attire appropriate for
one who rode in limousines and private jets. Attire
appropriate for a man about to fly through the heavens
and be plopped into the lap of Miss January St. John.

January, he thought. He'd dreamed about her again the previous night. He'd hoped he wouldn't do that so close to seeing her again, as his dreams were disturbing, to say the least. The night before, she had been wearing a sheer white, flowing gown that gave tantalizing hints of her lush body beneath. They'd been on a beach of some sort with misty fog hovering in the air. January had beckoned to him, smiled, held out her arms, and Houston had gone forward. But then she'd disappeared, leaving him holding the wispy gown in his hands.

Heat gathered low in Houston's body as he recalled the dream, and he shifted in his seat as he cleared his throat.

"Sir?" the driver asked.

"What? Oh, nothing," Houston said. Weird, he thought. Clearing his throat meant he was about to say something important to the driver? Hadn't they heard of a good old "Hey, you"? Oh, well, who understood the rich and famous? Rich, wealthy, megabucks . . . January. She sure hadn't acted like a rich snob that day at the institute. She'd plowed right in like a sandlot brawler. Really something. And later, too, at the police station, she hadn't strutted her stuff, announced to the world that she was a St. John. She'd been quiet and dignified, ignoring the flurry her name *had* caused, then conversed with her lawyer and the police officials. Houston and his father had been released, and off they'd gone to the airport in January's limo.

What had his father said about January? Houston pondered. Something about her being rich but not acting rich. Well said. Of course, sending a car and plane for him might be construed as acting rich.

But she'd been so casual about it, it was hard to find fault. There'd been no hint of superiority in her voice, no hesitation while she waited for his awed reaction. The plane was there, so she was making use of it, much like Houston tossing Dallas his keys and saying, "Take my truck."

Fascinating, Houston mused. But not important, really. How January dealt with being wealthy had nothing to do with him, because January, herself, was going to have nothing to do with him after this trip. She'd be out of his life, his head, his dreams. And it was about time! She'd driven him crazy for two months, and he was fed up with it.

He settled more comfortably into the plush seat and looked out the window. Yep. He really did like limousines.

January stood, sat down, then stood again. The pilot had gone into the terminal, and she was alone in the private jet. Alone, and she knew, darn it, that she was nervous.

But who wouldn't be? she reasoned. She was about to see the man who had had a tremendous impact on her life. A man she hadn't seen in two months but who never had been far from her thoughts. She could see him as clearly as though he were standing in front of her. And in a very short time he would be!

Calm down, she told herself. She was acting like a ninny. She was January St. John, for heaven's sake, who made decisions involving hundreds of thousands, even millions, of dollars.

But, she thought, that was money: Cold, unfeeling, nonhuman money. Houston Tyler was real; he was a man. Oh, was he ever a man. He was a man like none she had ever met before. He was a man—Enough. She had covered quite adequately the potent fact that Houston was a man.

January ran her damp hands over her faded jeans and took a steadying breath. She was fine now, just fine. Under control. Doing great. She also couldn't remember where she'd left her shoes.

"Darn," she said, peering under the seats. She spotted the loafers, put them on, then straightened the edge of the yellow T-shirt over the waistband of her jeans.

She had searched high and low in her huge closet for the faded jeans and casual top. Houston had come to one of the top-rated institutes in the country in jeans and a knit shirt. A knit shirt that had stretched across those broad shoulders, she mused. Clung to his muscled chest, banded his tight biceps and— No, forget that. She'd dressed in a manner that he could relate to, would make him feel comfortable, hopefully ease the effect of the private, luxury jet.

She gasped, as she heard the sound of a car approaching. She stood in the center of the plane and waited. She heard car doors open, close, a car being driven away. She heard the sound of someone climbing the metal steps to the plane. And she heard the wild thudding of her heart echoing in her ears.

Any second now. Any second, and through that door would come . . .

Houston.

He bent his head to enter, then straightened, after placing a small suitcase on the floor just inside the door. He glanced around with interest, then saw . . .

January.

Neither moved.

Eyes of brown met the gaze of eyes of gray, and neither moved.

Oh, no. Oh, no, no, no, January thought frantically. He was even bigger, and more beautiful, and exuded even more blatant masculinity than she remembered. No, no, no. This wasn't fair. How dare he be more handsome, more virile, more . . . everything. How dare he look at her like that with those great big brown eyes, pin her in place, melt her bones so she couldn't move.

Oh, hell, Houston thought, he was in deep trouble. He hadn't expected to see January on that plane, but there she was, and she was beautiful; more beautiful than his memories of her, and more beautiful than the vision who appeared in his dreams at night. Deep, deep trouble.

Footsteps clattered on the metal stairs, and both January and Houston jerked in surprise. A man entered the plane.

"All set, Miss St. John?" he asked.

"What? Yes, Terry, whenever you are. Oh, this is Houston Tyler. Houston, this is Terry Russell, our pilot."

The two men shook hands. "Buckle up, folks," Terry then said. "We have tower clearance to put this bird in the air." He pulled up the stairs, closed the door, and disappeared into the front of the plane.

"Houston?" January said, sweeping her arm toward a blue velveteen easy chair.

Houston sat down and adjusted his seat belt. January sat in the chair beside him and did the same. The engines came alive, rumbled, then the plane slowly began to move. January and Houston stared straight ahead, not looking at each other.

Dammit, Houston fumed. How was he going to get January St. John out of his system when all he could think about was what it would be like to haul her into his arms and kiss her? The reaction of his body confirmed the fact that he wanted to feel her in his arms, close, pressed against him where he could savor her softness, taste, aroma. This was not going the way he'd planned it at all.

The plane picked up speed as it went down the runway, then lifted off the ground and reached for the heavens.

She was going to get off, January thought irrationally. She was going to get up and politely take her leave. She couldn't handle the situation. She didn't know what to do. It had been Houston—the man, Houston, himself—who had caused the restlessness, the sense of something missing.

She wanted to kiss him. She wanted to run. She wanted to feel the steel bands of his arms gathering her to the hard wall of his body. She wanted to get off the plane! She'd gotten her answer, and she was scared to death.

"I didn't expect to see you here," Houston said softly, breaking the tense silence. He turned his head to look at her.

She met his gaze, her pulse skittering. "I decided to come at the last minute. I hope you don't mind."

He shrugged. "It's your plane."

"No, it's not," she said quickly. "I mean, it's not mine, per se. It belongs to the company."

"Your company?"

"No, no, my mother's. She took over after my father died. I'm just"—she waved a hand breezily in the air—"an employee, a worker, someone on the payroll like the rest of the crowd."

Houston shook his head. "Not quite."

"Oh, but I am. My mother would fire me in a minute if I didn't do my job correctly," January said. Oh, she would not. Sara St. John would help January see what she'd done wrong, then tell her to get back in there and try again. "Well, not fire me, maybe, but— Oh, never mind." She unfastened her seat belt, slipped off her shoes, and got to her feet. "Would you like something to drink? Coffee? Juice?"

"No thank you," Houston said, releasing his own seat belt. T-shirt, tight faded jeans, and bare feet. Beautiful. When he'd seen her two months ago, she'd been wearing a fancy blue suit with a pink silk blouse, and she'd been beautiful then too. He was surprised to see her dressed the way she was today. He didn't know rich people had faded jeans that hugged their delectable little bottoms and their long, long legs.

He cleared his throat as heat rocketed through the lower regions of his body.

"Yes?" January said.

Houston laughed. "Nothing. That's the second time today I've cleared my throat and was expected to say something of importance. Is that a rule in your part of society?"

January went behind a small bar and returned with a glass of orange juice. She sat down next to Houston again.

"My part of society?" she repeated, frowning slightly.

"The upper crust," he said. And he *had* to remember that. But, damn, it was hard to do when she was sitting there looking like she was going on an old-fashioned, middle-class picnic.

"You look rather upper-crust yourself," she said, her gaze flickering over his attire. "You could pass for a yuppie with no problem."

"And you look like you're going to plant a garden," he said, smiling at her.

"I did that once," she said, matching his smile. "My father helped me. I was, oh, seven or eight, I guess. I planted carrots, radishes, lettuce, all kinds of great veggies. Every morning I'd run outside to see if anything was growing."

"And?"

"A radish. All that work and the only thing that came up was one radish. My father made a ceremony out of slicing it up and dividing it between the three of us. I was so crushed. One radish. We never did figure out what went wrong."

"Was it a good radish?" Houston asked, still smiling.

"Blue-ribbon quality, sir. You know, years later my mother told me that my father had wanted to buy some vegetables and stick them in the ground. He couldn't bear to see me disappointed after I'd worked so hard. But my mother said no, that even children have to learn to deal with disappointment, with things not going the way they'd planned. She told my father he was solving my problems with money, by buying my feeling of accomplishment at the grocery store. She wanted me to see that money doesn't solve everything; it's people who count. And so, my garden produced one radish. I was very, very proud of that radish after I got over my initial upset."

"That's quite a story," Houston said, looking directly at her. "Your parents sound like remarkable people. You must miss your father very much."

"I do, and I know you understand that. It was apparent from what took place at the institute that you Tylers are very close."

"Very," he said, nodding.

"We're fortunate, Houston. It seems like everyone I grew up with is on their third or fourth stepmother or stepfather. What a lovely thing we have in common."

"Yeah."

A silence fell as they looked at each other. A silence charged with awareness, with currents of sexuality that seemed to weave back and forth between them. A silence that spun invisible silken threads that pulled at them, drew them closer, then even closer together . . .

January had the hazy sensation that she was standing outside of her body watching the scene before her. She saw Houston lift his large hand, slip it to the nape of her neck, then lean toward her, oh, so slowly.

Closer . . .

Houston felt as though he were drowning in the gray depths of January's big eyes. Gray, like the misty fog of his dream. Only this time it was real, and this time she wasn't going to disappear, and this time, after all these weeks, he was going to taste the sweetness of her mouth on his.

Closer . . .

A wondrous trembling swept through January, a sense of anticipation greater than any she had ever known. She could feel Houston's warm breath feathering over her lips, causing her heart to race. He was going to kiss her. He *had* to kiss her, before she died on the spot from the raging desire to feel his lips claim hers.

"Houston," she said, her voice a seductive whisper.

He lifted his other hand to cradle the side of her face and increased the pressure at the nape of her neck just enough to cause her to lean even more toward him.

And then he kissed her.

With gentle insistence he parted her lips, his tongue slipping inside to find hers. She lifted her hands to rest on his broad shoulders, feeling the hard, bunching muscles, savoring the strength and power beneath her palms. His mouth was soft, his tongue sweet torture. She drank of his taste, inhaled his aroma, felt the heated coil of her desire pulsing deep, so deep, inside her.

Houston felt the flames of passion lick through his body, gathering low, stirring his manhood. His tongue explored every hidden crevice of January's mouth, the ridge of her teeth, the seductive softness of her tongue as it dueled with his. Never had there been such a kiss. Never before had he registered such instant, driving want and need, the desire to become one, now, with a woman. Her scent was intoxicating, her mouth was an instrument of pleasure. January held the sensual promise of being all that was woman, and he wanted her. Blood pounded in his veins, and his breathing became rough. His muscles began to tremble from forced restraint, and he slowly, reluctantly, lifted his head.

January opened her eyes to stare into the brown pools of Houston's. He was still a breath away from her . . . so close, yet too far. She wanted him to kiss her again, fill her with that incredible heat, allow her to feel the shattering pleasure of his mouth, his tongue finding hers.

Houston drew his hands away and straightened, his gaze never leaving January's. He willed his body under control, resisted the temptation to claim her mouth once more. He hadn't planned to kiss her. He hadn't meant to kiss her. But now that he'd kissed her? Oh, Lord, he wanted to kiss her again.

He tore his gaze from hers, drew a steadying breath, and stared straight ahead. "I'm sorry," he said, his voice still raspy with passion. "I shouldn't have done that."

January blinked, sat back in her chair, and filled her lungs with air. "Why not?"

Because it was July, his mind thundered. Because he was supposed to be getting her out of his system, not aching to mesh them together as one entity.

"It was a mistake, January," he said, "and I apologize. It won't happen again."

It wouldn't? she thought desperately. He was never going to kiss her again? That was the most depressing thing she'd ever heard. It had been a wonderful kiss, a glorious kiss, and she wanted another. A dozen more. A zillion of Houston Tyler's kisses.

"I . . . I enjoyed that kiss, Houston," she said, looking at him.

Frowning, he met her gaze. "So did I. That's the problem. That's why I'm not going to kiss you again."

"There must be some logic there somewhere," January said, matching his frown, "but it escapes me. Would you care to explain?"

He pulled the knot of his tie down several inches. "No."

"Houston, why did you come on this trip?"

"Why did you ask me to come?" he shot back, his jaw tightening. "And don't give me the crock about every construction worker in New York City being busy."

"If you knew it," she said, her voice rising, "then why did you come?"

"That's none of your business. I'm here. I'll do the job you hired me to do. That's it," he said gruffly. And he would not, he told himself firmly, kiss her again. Not kiss her, or touch her, or get within ten feet of her.

"Why are you so angry?" she asked.

"I'm not angry," he yelled.

"Well, you could have fooled me," she said, getting to her feet. She stomped over to the bar and pulled a plate of sandwiches from the refrigerator. She plunked the plate on the counter, added a bowl of fruit, and two bottles of soda. "Lunch is ready," she said tightly.

Houston got to his feet, pulled his tie off, and stuffed it into his pocket. He went to the bar, sat on a stool, and looked at January, who was standing behind the counter.

"This isn't going very well," he said quietly. "I'll understand if you want to tell the pilot to turn around and take me back to Chicago."

"Is that what you want?" she asked softly. No! Oh, no. That wasn't what he wanted, was it? Then she'd never see him again. Not ever. Under the circumstances, because of the answer, she didn't know if she *should* be seeing him, but the thought of *never* seeing him—

"It would be the smart thing to do," he said, "but no, it's not what I want." Fool. Lord, he was an

idiot. He should put as much distance as possible
between them, as it was apparent that seeing January St. John again was not going to solve his problem. Now it was even worse because he'd kissed her.
Talk about deep trouble!

But, he mentally went on, this wouldn't be the
first time in his life he'd had to pull back, regroup,
start over. When Dallas had married Joyce and moved
to Arizona, Houston had had to face the fact that
their company, Tyler Construction, was a forgotten
dream.

Houston picked up a sandwich and took a bite.
So, he told himself, he'd come up with a new plan.
Since he now knew that seeing January wasn't going
to solve a thing, he needed to gather evidence that
would show him in no uncertain terms that she was
the wrong woman for him. But at the moment his
body didn't give a damn.

He needed, he decided, visible, tangible proof because his mind had a way of short-circuiting while
in the presence of January St. John. And his body?
Forget it. He didn't want to think about the condition of his body.

Houston polished off the sandwich, drank half a
bottle of soda, and reached for another sandwich.
Now then, he thought, what did he have so far?
Visible, tangible proof that January St. John was
out of his league, one of the untouchables. The limousine and the private jet. Good. Wrong. He really
liked that limousine, and this plane sure beat trying
to fold his big self into one of those seats on a
commercial flight.

And he'd already decided she'd handled the existence of the plane and limo with such casualness,

there was no fault to be found. Wonderful. On top of that, he was dressed to the teeth, while January was decked out like the farmer's daughter, including bare feet, for crying out loud. He was back to square one.

"Hell," he muttered, then reached for another sandwich.

"You don't like tuna?" January said. "I think there's some egg salad in this stack."

"What? Oh, no, this is fine. Very good. January, you never answered my question about why you asked me to come on this trip."

"And you never answered mine about why you came."

"We're playing games here," he said.

She sighed. "I know. I don't like games, and I don't like people who play them. I find it hard to believe I'm doing it myself, but I was desperate."

"What do you mean?"

January threw up her hands. "Oh, well, my pride be damned. Here it is in a nutshell. Houston, I've been off balance, not myself, for the past couple of months. I've felt restless, out of sorts. These new feelings came over me so close to the time that I met you that I wasn't sure if you were the cause."

"Me?" Shock was evident on his face.

"Yes. Was the timing just a coincidence, or was it because . . . because you had touched my life? I didn't know, but I had to know. I was going crazy, so I made up the story about there being no one to look at the house on the island. Well, now that my pride is totally in shreds, it's your turn. Why did you come when you knew I could have found someone in New York to do the job?"

"I'll be damned," Houston repeated, staring at her.

"So you're trying to solve a problem within yourself
you're looking for the answer."

No, darn it, she thought, she knew the answer
now. The next stumbling block was what she was
going to do about it.

"Something like that," she said.

"I'll be damned."

"Quit saying that, and tell me why you came."

"Okay," he said, nodding. "Fair is fair, pride be
damned. I haven't been able to get you off my mind
since I met you."

"Really?" she said, smiling. Really? Oh, how marvelous! He'd been thinking about her for the past
two months, just as she'd been thinking of him.

"I'm not a stupid man, January. I know we come
from different worlds. We have nothing in common,
don't operate on the same social level. Even knowing
we don't belong together, I couldn't forget you. So I
decided to see you again to . . . well, get you out of
my system. That's why I came on this trip."

"Oh," she said, frowning. "You want me out of
your system? That's not very flattering, Houston."

"But it's the only way, don't you see? January,
face facts. We come from two different worlds. Instead of looking for your answer, you should be
concentrating on how to get me off your mind. The
answer isn't important. What matters is that we've
somehow taken up residency in each other's heads,
and it's screwing up our chances at finding happiness with other people."

"Other people?" she said, leaning toward him.
"What other people?"

"The ones we'll each discover in our own worlds
once we clear up this mess."

"Mess?"

"Come on, don't be dense. What would your mother say if she knew you were preoccupied with thoughts of a construction worker? It won't work, *we* won't work, and we both know it."

Houston Tyler, January thought, hiding her smile, was underestimating Sara St. John. And, by gum, he was underestimating January St. John. So! Houston was here, on this plane, because he'd been thrown for a loop when they'd met, just as she had. Incredible.

"January?" Houston said, pulling her from her thoughts.

"Yes?"

"Look, pride or not, I'm glad we were up-front about this. Now we can help each other."

"We can?"

"Sure. See, what we have here is a very strong physical attraction. On an intellectual level we know we're not suited for each other, but biological urges can be heavy-duty."

"Houston, that's disgusting."

"It is not. It's fact. Take that kiss we shared, for example."

"Mmm," January said dreamily.

"Yeah," he said, staring into space. He snapped himself back to attention. "Anyway, what we need to do is spend some time together to prove to ourselves that our lifestyles, our backgrounds, the whole nine yards, are just too far apart. Telling ourselves that obviously isn't doing the job. We have to live it a bit."

"Good idea," she said brightly. "My, my, you're smart. If the institute knew about you, they'd be after you just like they're after Austin."

"I'm not *that* smart. Then we agree? We're going to help each other with this?"

She was playing games again, January realized. She really hated games, but she had no choice. This was a unique situation. She had to have the time she needed.

"As I mentioned," she said. "I think our spending time together is an excellent idea." There. She hadn't lied. She'd just wiggled around the truth a tad.

"Great, because I'm on a schedule."

"You're what?"

"July is my month. I've made up my mind to find the woman of my dreams and marry her. But first I have to be free of the hold you have on me, January. Get it?"

What *he* was going to get was another broken nose! No, that wasn't fair. Houston believed she was in total agreement that they were a mismatched couple. They weren't, not on the basis of background and finances, as she didn't care diddly about that stuff. It was the messages from her heart that she needed time to listen to.

"I've never heard of anyone putting aside a month to fall in love or whatever," she said.

"I'm determined, My whole family is paired off, month by month. July is mine. It'll be my birthday present to myself."

"Your birthday is in July?"

"Yeah," he said, "the thirty-first. I guess you were born in January."

"No-o-o," she said slowly, "I wasn't. My birthday, Mr. Tyler, is on July thirty-first."

Houston blinked. "What?"

January plunked her elbow on the bar, rested her

chin on her hand, and adopted an expression of pure innocence. "Isn't that something? Here we've already established the fact that we have loving families in common, and now this, the same birthday. July thirty-first. That is just so-o-o amazing. Houston?"

"What?" he said, appearing rather stunned.

"Would you like a piece of cake for dessert?"

"Cake? Oh, yes, if it's not any trouble."

"Not at all," she said, turning to the refrigerator. "My secretary had this ordered for the plane when I told her I was making this trip. She knows it's my favorite kind."

"My favorite . . ." Houston started absently, then stopped speaking as he stared at the slice of cake on the plate that January set in front of him. ". . . is marble," he finished. His voice sounded rather strangled as his gaze remained riveted on the cake.

January leaned over and peered at the dessert in front of him. "No kidding? White and chocolate swirled together like that is? Well," she said, patting his hand, "then I'm sure you'll enjoy it."

Houston just sat there, staring at the plate as though he'd never seen a piece of marble cake before in his entire life.

Three

Due to a series of unforeseen delays, it was late afternoon before January and Houston arrived in the small town on the coast of Maine.

A sudden and violent storm had forced Terry, the pilot, to radio for clearance to move into a different traffic pattern in the turbulent sky. Permission granted, he flew in a wider, higher approach to the airfield they sought, only to be told he would have to go farther, as no planes could land in the fog that had settled in after the storm.

Unfortunately the car that January had arranged to meet them was at the first airport. At last on the ground, January spoke to the only clerk on duty in the small terminal about renting a car. The elderly man scratched his head, said, "They didn't have none of them fancy rent-a-car things," but his grandson had a pickup truck he might be willing to rent out if the price was right. January looked at Houston, shrugged, then told the man they'd agree to

take the truck, sight unseen. Terry wished them
good luck, said he'd meet them at the airport at
noon the next day, then headed off to find a room
for the night.

The expression of shock on January's face when
the clanking vehicle came roaring up was, to Houston, absolutely priceless. He whooped with laughter,
told January she didn't appreciate vintage pickups,
and was rewarded with a murderous glare from Miss
St. John. Houston volunteered to drive. January
voiced no objection.

The thirty-mile trip was slow going over a bumpy,
muddy road. January held on for dear life, kept her
eyes closed a great deal of the time, and informed
Houston that his nose was in danger if he laughed
one more time. He hooted in delight. The sound was
infectious, and January was soon laughing right
along with him. Why she was laughing, she told
him, she had no idea, considering the fact that her
life was in jeopardy. Houston silently marveled at
the way she was taking the less-than-first-class trans-
portation in stride.

Things got worse. By the time they arrived in the
small fishing town that had been their destination,
the storm had shifted, dumping sheets of pelting
rain. Fog was rolling in off the water like marshmal-
lows, and the captain of the boat who was to take
January and Houston to the island said he couldn't
put it out in such weather. Soaked to the skin and
chilled to the bone from the sudden drop in temperature, the pair hurried to the only inn, in the center
of the three-block town.

"Only have one room," the woman behind the
counter said. "Fishermen in town, you know."

"We'll take it," January said, her teeth chattering. "Whatever it is, we'll take it."

"Best get your wife in a hot tub," the woman said to Houston, " 'fore she catches a chill."

"I'll see to it personally," Houston said, smiling as he accepted the key. "Come along, dear," he said to January as he picked up their suitcases. "We can't have you catching a chill. The children would never forgive me if I brought you home with a runny nose."

"Nose?" January said, smiling ever so sweetly. "Did you mention nose? Funny you should bring that up . . . dear."

Houston laughed, the woman behind the counter appeared totally confused, and January hurried toward the stairs leading to the second floor.

The room was decorated in blue and white with an old-fashioned four-poster bed, two easy chairs in front of a fireplace, a dresser, and a blue-and-white braided rug on a gleaming hardwood floor. White eyelet curtains hung at the windows.

"Oh, isn't this adorable?" January said.

"Bath. Now," Houston said. "You're shaking all over."

"You're right, I'm freezing," she said. She opened her suitcase, pulled out dry clothes, and headed for the bathroom. "I'll hurry. You're just as wet and cold."

"No rush. I have a bigger body, therefore more body heat."

"That's not one of the brightest things you've ever said," she shot back over her shoulder before disappearing into the bathroom.

Houston chuckled softly, then peeled off his sodden sport coat, placing it on a hanger in the closet.

He removed his shoes and socks and his wet shirt.
There was wood in the small fireplace, and he lit it
into a warming fire, rubbing his hands together in
front of the flames.

What a day, he mused. What an incredible day.
And January St. John was an incredible woman.
Not one of the women he knew, not one, would have
stood for the delays and discomfort he and January
had been through without whining and complain-
ing. But January? She'd simply smiled and laughed,
said it was an adventure of sorts, and had even
taken the time to admire the decor of the room.

The room. He turned slowly to look at it again.
One bed. One old-fashioned, cozy, made-for-two-
people bed.

Houston shook his head and turned back to the
fire. Forget it, Tyler, he told himself. There were also
two chairs that could be shoved together, and that
was where he would spend the night. While January
was in the bed. Just a few feet away. Wearing a filmy
gown like the one in his dream? Oh, Lord.

Knock it off, he admonished himself, as he felt a
shaft of heat shoot across his loins. Due to his and
January's up-front conversation, they were on the
same wavelength, shared the same goal. They would
help each other break free of the strange, unexplain-
able, invisible web that had fallen over them at their
meeting two months before. They both knew they
were not meant to have a relationship, that they
came from vastly different worlds, had nothing in
common.

Nothing in common, Houston's mind echoed. Except having been raised by loving families, sharing
the same birthday, selecting as their favorite a not

very common type of cake. Nothing in common but the ability to laugh right out loud while driving in a rattling pickup truck. Nothing in common but the sharing of a kiss that had set their blood on fire and sent their passions soaring.

Where, he wondered, was the flip side of the coin in his mind, the glaring reasons why he and January were not meant to be? It wasn't like him to view things through rose-colored glasses. He looked at life as it was, not as a pessimist, nor as an ostrichlike optimist, but as someone who was realistic, practical, and accepted facts as they were presented to him.

But with January, at that moment in time, he admitted, he was peering with tunnel vision. And it was all just so damn good. This wasn't like him at all, not at all, and it had to stop.

Houston looked around the room again. This was part of his problem, he reasoned. This room was a replica of another era. He was a captain home at last from months of sailing the high seas in a tall ship. There was a fire in the hearth, the four-poster bed was waiting for him to carry his lady to its haven and make love to her. It was as though he and January had been transported to another time and place. He was Captain Tyler of the mighty ship—

The bathroom door opened and January stepped out. Houston turned to look at her, saw the long, rose-colored velour robe she wore, the flush on her cheeks from the heat of her bath, saw her looking at him with eyes as gray as the misty fog that shut out the world beyond their room. The blood pounded in his veins.

Words formed in January's mind, telling Houston

that the bathroom was free, the hot water heavenly. Telling him how nice it was that he'd lit the welcoming fire. But she couldn't speak. Her lips were slightly parted, but no sound came. She could only look at Houston Tyler and drink in the sight of him, memorizing every detail.

The glow of the fire cast changing colors over his bare chest that was roped in muscles and covered in curly auburn hair. The thick hair on his head was shifting shades of mahogany and cinnamon and chestnuts. His shoulders and arms were beautifully proportioned in well-defined muscles that complimented his chest, narrow hips, and long, long legs.

He was the most magnificent man she had ever seen.

Whispers of heat crept through January, settling low in her belly in a deep, secret place; pulsing, aching with a sweet pain of the awareness of her own femininity. She was woman, and there, before her, was the epitome of man. Houston. He hadn't moved or spoken, the quiet power of his massive body seeming to call to her, only her.

On trembling legs she moved slowly forward, her gaze never leaving Houston's as he watched her come to him. She stopped in front of him and lifted shaking hands to his chest, weaving her fingers through the moist auburn curls. She felt his shudder of response as her palms skimmed over his nipples, then she stood on tiptoe to twine her arms around his neck and press her body to his.

With a groan that rumbled from deep in his throat, Houston wrapped his arms around her to bring her closer yet, then his mouth melted over hers.

The kiss was urgent frenzied, hungry. It was

tongues meeting, dueling, tasting. Their bodies strained against each other in a need to feel every inch of the one in their embrace. The fire crackled in the hearth, and a fire of passion swept through them. Waves of desire pounded against their senses like the waves on the shore beyond the room, the tempestuous rhythm of raging desire causing a roaring noise in their ears like the wind of nature's gale.

Houston's large hands roamed over the fleecy material of January's robe, knowing she was naked beneath it. He cupped her buttocks and spread his legs slightly to nestle her to the cradle of his hips. His manhood surged against the zipper of his slacks; heavy, heated, aching for release that only the honeyed warmth of January's body could give him.

Dear heaven, his mind thundered, how he wanted this woman! Never before, never, had he been filled with such driving want and need. It was consuming him, pushing aside his control, his sense of reason and reality. There was only this hot, burning fire. There was only January.

January clung to Houston for support as she answered the demands of his lips and tongue in total abandon. The empty, chilling void within her of the past two months was filled with indescribable joy, heat, and sensations like none she had ever experienced before. Desire thrummed deep within her, like a liquid fire that only Houston could quell. The answer was found, the answer was Houston, and she wanted him, all of him. Their joining would be a celebration, a union of splendor. Two months of waiting . . . two months . . . and oh, how she wanted him.

Houston lifted his head to draw air into his lungs,

his breathing labored. He trailed light, nibbling kisses down January's throat as she tilted her head back to give him access to the sensitive, dewy softness of her skin.

"Houston, please," she whispered.

Her plea slammed against his mind as he felt a tremor course through her body. "Houston, please," he heard again and again, pulling him back from the haze of passion where he had gone. Reality edged in around the mist, dimming the image of the sea captain, his lady, and the tall ship. He heard the pounding of his own heart, the rasp of his breathing, the fire crackling in the hearth. The room tilted, blurred in his vision, steadied, then came into crystal-clear focus in the here and now.

He stiffened. He saw January's kiss-swollen lips, the flush of passion on her cheeks, the smoky hue of desire in her gray eyes as she slowly lifted her lashes to meet his gaze.

"Dear God," he said, his voice gritty. "What am I doing?" He gently pulled her arms from his neck, then took a step backward as he drew a shuddering breath.

"Houston?" January said, swaying slightly on her feet.

'Houston, please,' echoed in his mind. She had begged him to stop. Had he frightened her? Hurt her? What had happened to him? He'd never lost control like that before.

He stared at the ceiling for a long moment, gathering his control, fighting against the urge to sweep her into his arms and carry her to the bed where he would thrust deep within her, make them one. He slowly met her gaze again.

"January, I—"

"Why did you stop? I thought you wanted me."

"What?" he asked, raking a restless hand through his hair.

January took a step backward and wrapped her hands around her elbows. "Well, I guess not," she said, attempting a smile that didn't materialize. "My mistake."

"January, you don't understand," he said, reaching for her. She backed up further, and he dropped his hand to his side.

"It's better this way," she said, hating the quavering of her voice. "I mean, after all, we're on a campaign to forget each other, right?" Oh, God, she was going to cry. She'd never forgive herself again if she cried. "It wouldn't be very smart to make love with me, because I'm supposed to be exiting your system, or whatever. Of course, you didn't want me, that makes sense. I mean, your body wanted me, but your mind knew better. Aren't we lucky that you have such a marvelous mind? Otherwise, we might have—"

"January, stop it," Houston said sharply.

"You weren't kidding when you said that biological urges were heavy-duty. Mercy. They are really something. Yes, siree bob, they are—"

He closed the distance between them and gripped her upper arms. "Hush!" he ordered, a muscle jumping along his jaw.

"Well, I'm right, aren't I?" she asked, willing herself not to cry. "It would have been a mistake. We're supposed to be spending time together to prove how wrong we are for each other. Making love, going to bed together, would have just complicated the issue. Right? Right, Houston?"

"Yeah, right," he said quietly, releasing her arms. "Why do you look like you're about to cry?"

"Me? Oh. Well, because I'm tired and hungry. It's been a long day. I'll dress while you shower, then we can see about dinner. Okay?"

He studied her face as she managed a small smile. Finally he nodded, then opened his suitcase, took out some clothes, and went into the bathroom, closing the door behind him.

January sank onto one of the chairs and pressed her fingertips to her lips. Two tears slid down her cheeks. She brushed them angrily away, then got to her feet.

When she blew her pride all to hell, she thought ruefully, she didn't mess around. First on the plane when she'd told Houston how unsettled she'd been for the past two months, and now in this room. "Houston, please," she'd begged, wanting him so much, needing to be one with him. And it hadn't been just biological urges . . . Lord, she hated how that sounded. . . . Emotions had been involved, needs of her heart and mind, her soul as well.

Was she falling in love with Houston Tyler?

Falling in love with a man who was determined to evict her from his mind, anxious to get rid of her so he could find the woman of his dreams, staying on his damnable schedule? July was his month, he'd said. Well, phooey on that. She had a claim on July too. Her birthday was the same as his, and she could do with *her* July whatever she darn well pleased.

For example, she mused, she could fall totally,

completely, absolutely head over heels in love with Houston Tyler.

Which would be the dumbest, most idiotic thing she'd ever done.

Because he didn't want any part of her. The nincompoop.

Well, she mentally rambled on as she pulled on bikini panties and a matching bra. He *did* want a part of her . . . her luscious body. She'd been molded to him, plastered against him, and certain parts of *his* anatomy didn't lie. What he *didn't* want was her person, her self, her existence in his life as a total woman. He'd probably be only too happy to make love with her, but he didn't want to fall *in* love.

And January St. John, she asked herself as she finished dressing in gray slacks and a gray-and-white cashmere sweater, what did she want? More to the point, did she have a choice? Somehow she didn't think so. She had a feeling that if she was going to fall in love with Houston, there wouldn't be a thing she could do to stop it. Nor could she do anything about the guaranteed broken heart that love would bring her because she wouldn't be loved in return. What a raw deal. Well, one thing was for certain. If she *did* fall in love with Houston, he'd never know it. The least she could do was hang on to the last shard or two of her shattered pride.

January retrieved her hairbrush from her suitcase and went to the mirror that hung above the old-fashioned dresser. She flicked her dark curls around her face, then leaned closer to peer at her reflection.

She looked, she decided, like a woman who had been very thoroughly and very expertly kissed. There was a rosy hue to her lips that wasn't normally there, a glow to her skin, a sparkle in her eyes that spoke of secret pleasures.

She leaned closer. All that in one little face? she wondered. Yep, sure enough, there it all was. Mercy, she certainly hoped no one they saw at dinner was into face reading, if there was such a thing. What would Houston see when he looked at her? Well, he knew she'd been kissed because he was the kisser who had transformed her, the kissee—was that how that went?—into this transparent creature who was advertising exactly what she'd been doing.

January tilted her head from side to side, glimpsing her face from different angles. Strange, she mused. She'd been kissed before, but she'd never looked like *this*.

The bathroom door snapped opened, startling January so badly that she spun around with a gasp and flung the hairbrush in the direction of the noise in reflex to her momentary fright. The brush bounced off the hard wall of Houston's chest and landed with a thud on the floor.

Houston's mouth dropped opened as he looked at January, then stared at the hairbrush. She absently registered the fact that he looked marvelous in jeans and a dark brown sweater, then her eyes riveted on the brush.

"Sorry," she mumbled.

"You forgot I was here?" he said, raising his eyebrows.

Not a chance, January thought. He was there, all right. All she had to do was look in the mirror to remember just how "there" he had been.

And then she laughed.

She laughed because she was still a breath away from crying, and she had no intention of crying in front of Houston. She laughed because she was tired and hungry, and because her nerves were shot and her emotions stretched to the limit. She laughed because the remembrance of her hairbrush bouncing off Houston's chest was actually pretty funny.

And so she laughed.

She laughed until she could hardly breathe and had to sink onto the edge of the bed, wrapping her arms around her stomach. Houston crossed his arms over his chest and watched, a rather bland, pleasant expression on his face.

"Oh, my," she said finally. "Goodness." She wiped tears of merriment from her cheeks.

"Finished?" he asked calmly.

"What? Oh, well, yes, I guess so. Sorry 'bout that. It was"—she shrugged, then threw up her hands—"funny."

"Obviously. January, there were a mother and a sister in the house while I was growing up. I decided early on that the female species is fascinating, enchanting. But I also realized that if I lived to be a hundred, I would never, ever, understand women. Shall we go see if we can find some dinner?"

Had she been insulted? January wondered. She was too hungry to worry about it. "Certainly," she said. She swished past him, tilting her nose in the air just in case she *had* been insulted.

Houston's low, sexy chuckle deflated her flouncing exit and caused a shiver to dance along her spine.

The inn had a small dining room boasting a roar

ing fire in the hearth, rough-cut wood tables and benches, and two waitresses dressed in costumes depicting the era of the pubs on the waterfront.

Captain Tyler now took his lady to dinner, Houston thought, being prepared to protect her from the rowdy sailors who had spent months at sea on the tall ships. Wonderful. He was slipping over the edge, totally losing his mind.

They sat at a table near the fire and ordered clam chowder and homemade bread. January stared into the flames.

So beautiful, Houston mused. And in his arms she was heaven itself. Kissing January St. John made his blood run hotter than that fire in the hearth. How much of that burning desire for her had been real, and what had been a product of his fanciful thoughts of tall ships and sea captains? He had a feeling it had all been real, all been January. And that was *not* good. He was falling backward, losing ground in his goal to be free of the strange hold she had on him.

At that moment, he knew, he didn't want to be free of her. He wanted to haul her into his arms, kiss her, then make love to her in the four-poster bed.

Houston glanced around the room as the waitress set their dinners in front of them. He saw two couples, but the rest were men, and he caught snatches of conversation of what fish they had caught and the ones that had gotten away. They were on vacation, he supposed, escaping from their hectic lives, just kicking back and enjoying themselves.

Escaping, his mind repeated. Yes, this was certainly the place to do that, especially now with the

fog enclosing them, shutting them off from the out
side world. It was as though they were all removed
from reality.

"Mmm, this is delicious," January said.

He picked up his spoon and sampled the chowder
"You're right." They ate in silence for several min
utes. "January," he said finally, "about what hap
pened in the room. I—"

"I'd rather just forget it," she said, not meeting
his gaze. She buttered a slice of bread.

"Look, all I'm trying to say is," Houston went on
"this place, the weather, the whole bit, isn't normal."

"Well, it isn't weird. This is a lovely inn, and the
people are very nice."

"What I mean is, it's not the world you normally
live in. You're high-society, big-finance Manhattan."

"So?"

"So everyone is in the same boat here. We're caught
by fog, held in place, almost like we've been dropped
back in history to the days of pubs and sailing ships."

"Houston, this is not *The Twilight Zone*. There's
a despicable pickup truck outside that says we are
still in the eighties. What is your point?"

"The point is," he said, leaning toward her, "tha
here we're just a man and a woman, nothing more."

"Sounds good to me," January said breezily. "Wan
some bread?"

"Thank you," he said, accepting the thick slice
"January, it *isn't* good. It's too easy to forget tha
there are tremendous differences in our lifestyles
our—"

"Yes, yes," she said, interrupting, "I've heard al
that."

"And we can't forget it. We can't get caught up in this atmosphere and forget that we have a goal."

"Your system," she said, frowning.

"*Our* system, remember? You want to be free too. We agreed on that. All I'm saying is, we have to be careful. What happened upstairs is evidence of how strong our—"

"So help me, Houston Tyler, if you say 'biological urges,' I won't be responsible for the condition of your nose."

"Well, what would you call what happened?"

Delicious, January thought dreamily. Until he'd turned her down flat. "Do we have to discuss this?"

"I think it's important that we're aware of . . . do you feel all right? You didn't get sick from being so cold and wet, did you? Your skin is sort of flushed and your eyes are . . . I don't know. They look different."

Oh, mercy, January thought frantically, he'd read her face! He'd actually done it. She ought to open her mouth and say, "Actually, Houston, honey pie, this face before you is a result of your kissing the living daylights out of me." Instead she said, "I'm fine."

"Well, if you're sure. Where was I?'

January sighed. "Trying to remember we're not normal, or that we *are* normal. I don't know. You lost me back in *The Twilight Zone*. Okay, let's see. This is not New York, I don't have a bunch of money to haul around in a wheelbarrow, so it's not helping the cause."

"Right. There's no tangible, visible proof of our differences."

The man-and-woman differences, January thought

merrily, had gotten very tangible and visible up in their room. "Right," she said firmly.

"Then we agree that we have to stay alert, no succumb to the circumstances."

"Sir," she said, covering her heart with her hand "do I appear to be the type of woman who suc cumbs? Really!" She sniffed indignantly for goo measure.

"Would you get serious?" he said, glaring at her.

"Well, good grief, Houston, you act as though we'r going to be here for a month. Tomorrow we'll go t the island, then fly back to New York."

"I live in Chicago, remember?"

"True, but you should witness me doing my mone thing in Manhattan, right?"

"Good thought," he said, nodding.

Time, January mused. She was gaining time; hou by hour, minute by minute. Time with Houston Was it hopeless? Was it? Would she have enough time to discover her true feelings for him? And she did hear the message of love from her heart would being a January, ready to receive that love really matter? Houston was determined to get he out of his life. Was there any chance at all that h might come to love her? Oh, for Pete's sake, how had she gotten herself into such a rotten mess?

"Miss St. John?" the waitress said.

"Yes?"

"This phone message came for you," the woma said, handing January a piece of paper.

"Thank you," she said. She quickly read the note "Oh, that's . . . interesting."

"What is?"

"It's from Terry. He's in the other town, you know

He said tomorrow is the Fourth of July, and there are big celebrations planned. He'll wait for my message at the inn where's he's staying, but he doubts if anyone will take us to the island tomorrow."

Houston got to his feet. "I'll go check."

"Okey-dokey," she said, then smiled before she took a big bite of bread and butter.

Houston hesitated, narrowed his eyes at her, but January just chewed. He left the room and returned a few minutes later.

"Terry is right," he said after sitting back down. "Tomorrow is one big party. We can't get to the island." Damn.

"Oh," January said. Hooray! she thought.

Another night, Houston thought. Another night in that room upstairs with January. Oh, Lord, he wasn't going to survive this.

"Houston, can't we just relax a little? So, okay, this isn't how either of us usually exists, but can't we enjoy it as long as we're here?"

"Dangerous."

"If we stay alert like you said? You don't know how alert I can be once I've made up my mind to be alert. I'll tell myself fifty times a day that I'm filthy rich so I won't forget. Come on, lighten up. Just think, an old-fashioned Fourth-of-July celebration. It'll be fun." She leaned toward him. "Okay?"

Houston groaned inwardly. When she looked at him like that, he'd agree to anything. He'd give her the moon, the stars, the sun. She wanted the Fourth of July? He'd take her into his arms and create fireworks that she wouldn't believe. He'd— Enough. "Yeah, okay," he said, concentrating on the last of his chowder.

"Great," she said, then slathered another slice of bread with butter. Time, she thought. Minute by minute, hour by hour . . . time. With Houston.

After huge servings of apple pie topped by slabs of cheese, January groaned. "Oh, I'm stuffed." She glanced at the ceiling. "The rain has stopped. Could we go for a walk to work off some of this dinner?"

"Sure," Houston said, "as long as we don't go too far if it's still foggy. I have no wish to spend the night lost out there somewhere." He signaled to the waitress.

What *were* his wishes for the night? January wondered. Did he think about making love to her? Or was it the furthest thing from his mind since dismissing their kiss as a biological urge and a mistake? What was going on in that brain beneath that yummy auburn hair?

Nice goin', Tyler, Houston thought. He just had to mention the night ahead. The very image in his mind of trying to sleep in the same room with January without touching her was enough to make him grind his teeth in agony. He'd probably have an easier time of it lost in the fog.

The waitress placed the bill on the table. "Have a nice night," she said.

Ha! January thought.

Hell! Houston thought.

He reached for the bill as January did, his hand covering hers on top of the paper.

"This is part of the travel expenses, Houston," she said. "So is the room. St. John Enterprises will pay for it." Darn, darn. It was some of Houston's ever-famous tangible, visible proof of her money.

Houston frowned. How did he feel about this? he

asked himself. He'd had lunch with a woman architect a few months ago to discuss some plans, and she'd picked up the tab. Business expenses were business expenses. It didn't matter if they were a man's or a woman's. It wasn't a situation that was unique to a St. John, it took place thousands of times a day across the country. No big deal.

He met January's gaze. "Your check." He didn't remove his hand from hers as he stroked her soft skin with his thumb. "Business expense."

"Yes," she said, exhaling a little puff of air.

The heat from Houston's hand was traveling up her arm and across her breasts, causing them to feel heavy, achy, needing the soothing magic of his touch. The heat went lower, spiraling down deep. Desire. Desire so strong, it seemed to be stealing the very breath from her body. Desire that was changing the sparkling brown of Houston's eyes to smoky pools radiating a message as clear as the one thrumming within her.

Oh, yes, January thought dreamily, still ahead of them was the night. The two of them. Alone. In that room upstairs. January and Houston. Woman and man. It would be ecstasy.

". . . Do you want to?" Houston was saying.

"Oh-h-h, yes," she said with a sigh.

"Then I'll go up and get our coats."

January blinked. "What?"

"You just said you still wanted to go for a walk."

"I did? Oh, of course I did. Yes, you get the coats while I sign this bill."

"You're acting weird," he said, frowning.

"My brain gets muddled when my stomach is too

full. I have a wacky metabolism or . . . whatever."
She smiled brightly.

Houston shook his head, got to his feet, and left
the room. January pressed her hand to her forehead
to check her temperature.

There she'd sat, she thought incredulously, daydreaming about making love with a man whose chief
mission in life was to get her out of his mind and
his existence. She didn't take lovemaking lightly,
and there had been few, very few, men with whom
she'd wanted to share that intimate act.

But Houston Tyler? She knew, just somehow knew,
that becoming one with him would be special, rare,
beautiful, like nothing she'd experienced before. And,
darn it, he was wrong. There was more happening
between them than just physical chemistry, the god-
awful biological urges, and they owed it to themselves to discover exactly what it was. And *soon!*
Because confusion was totally exhausting.

Tonight, she thought decisively, was the night!

Four

Tonight, January thought glumly hours later, was *not* the night. There she was, trying to find a comfortable position in which to sleep on the two easy chairs, wiggling around, tossing and turning, in a pitch-black room . . . alone.

Well, she decided, it probably served her right. She had never in her life set out with the firm determination to make love with a man on the night *she* had chosen. To have been deposited by said man in their room while he beat a hasty retreat was, no doubt, her just desserts for her would-be wanton behavior. That did not, however, diminish her fervent wish to strangle Houston Tyler with her bare hands!

January punched the pillow and pulled the blanket up to her chin. The walk had been a dud, she mused. The fog was so thick, they couldn't see three feet in front of them. The air was chilly and damp, and within fifteen minutes they were back by the fire in the dining room of the inn.

They had joined in some general conversation with the other guests, but when Houston said he didn't like to fish, the other men, while polite, couldn't find anything to talk to him about.

Deciding the scene had been custom-ordered for her, January had feigned several loud yawns until Houston paid attention and suggested it was time to turn in. January had climbed the stairs on trembling legs, Houston behind her. The butterflies swooshing in her stomach felt as big as sea gulls, but when they stepped into the room, she knew without any reservation that she wanted Houston Tyler, wanted to make love with him, wanted to be one with him.

But Houston Tyler, the rat fink, had other ideas.

He had lit a fresh fire in the hearth, told January to take the bed as he would be fine on the two chairs pushed together, wished her a pleasant night's sleep, then . . . *poof!* He'd inched his way to the door and was gone.

January had stood with her mouth open, staring at the door in shock. Then had come a wave of icy misery as she realized that Houston had nearly fallen over his feet to get away from her. And then anger. Rip-roaring, mad-as-hell anger.

January had muttered under her breath the entire time she'd prepared for bed. How dare Houston kiss her until she was trembling in his arms, then dismiss it as a mistake. That was insensitive and rude. Kissing January St. John wasn't a mistake, it was an event, a happening, an experience. She didn't go around kissing every man who crossed her path, and Houston should consider himself a lucky so-and-so to be among the chosen few.

January wiggled again, then sniffled. She dismissed the idea of crying, as she wasn't in the mood to cry. She was pouting, whether her mother approved of St. Johns pouting or not. She was pouting as proficiently as any four-year-old and feeling terribly sorry for herself.

The fire had gone out, the room was as dark as soot, the chairs were horribly uncomfortable, and Houston Tyler didn't want to make love to her!

"Oh-h-h," she said with a moan, "I can't stand him." She should go get into the bed, she thought. When she'd pushed the chairs together, she'd realized that there was no way that Houston would come remotely close to fitting on them. So she'd found a blanket and pillow on the closet shelf and crawled onto the chairs herself. Well, no more Mr. Nice Guy. She was going over to the bed. No, she wasn't. Houston would be a twisted pretzel if he tried to sleep on those chairs. Why was she worried about him? He certainly didn't care diddly about her.

Why was she concerned about him? She asked herself again. Because she couldn't help it. Because he was Houston—great, big, beautiful Houston, who made her heart pound with his smile or a word spoken in that deep, rumbly voice. Because he melted her right down to her socks with his touch and made her ache with desire when he held and kissed her.

Because he was Houston Tyler.

An unknown emotion had been planted within her on the day she'd met Houston at the institute. In the two months since then, she now knew, it had grown, demanding her attention in ways she had not understood, in the form of her restlessness and the sense of something missing from her life. And now, she mused, the flower of that still unnamed emotion was in full bloom, the last petals opening as she'd stepped into Houston's embrace and felt his lips on hers. Was she really falling in love with Houston Tyler?

January crossed her arms over her breasts and stared up at a ceiling she couldn't see in the darkness.

All right, facts were facts, she thought. Houston was determined to prove they were wrong for each other. Well, she was determined to prove that they weren't. The battle lines were drawn. The war was on!

What if . . . oh, Lord, what if Houston's attraction to her *was* only physical? What if he felt nothing at all for her on an emotional level? What if she fought hard, won, proved to Houston that their worlds could mesh, only to discover that he had no depth of feeling for her, that he really didn't care?

No, no, no, January thought frantically, she wouldn't think about that now. That would have to go on a mental shelf for the time being before she blew a fuse in her brain. First things first. She had to show Houston that she was a woman, pure and simple, her last name and wealth be damned. And she mustn't cheat. Darn it.

She closed her eyes, drew one more deep, wobbly breath, then slept.

Houston stared moodily into the flames in the fireplace in the dining room, shutting out the buzz of voices in the background. He glanced at his watch, shook his head, then redirected his gaze to the fire.

He'd been sitting there for two hours, sending mental messages to January to go to sleep. Sound asleep. The kind of sleep that would take an earthquake to disturb. He wanted her dead to the world before he went back into that room.

He wanted, he repeated to himself, to make love to January St. John. For the past two hours he'd been taunted by her image as he'd stared into the fire. He could see her so clearly, hear her laughter, remember her aroma and the sweet taste of her mouth moving under his. His body tightened at the memory of January's soft curves molded to him as she'd returned his kiss in passionate abandon.

He hadn't dared, he knew, stay in that room with her when they'd gone upstairs. He'd literally dumped her inside and headed for the door. Just as he'd been about to close the door behind him, he'd glanced back at her, seen the shock on her face and what had appeared to be a flicker of pain, hurt, in her eyes. It had taken every ounce of willpower he had not to retrace his steps and pull her into his arms.

January.

January St. John, he thought, who had driven him nuts for two months and who was now turning him inside out and backward. He was a total wreck. He had no evidence so far, nothing to use to show they were wrong for each other. Every set of circumstances that had come up to reflect her wealth and, therefore, their glaring differences, he'd rationalized away. He had no defense against her sunshine smile, her unaffected ways, her natural beauty, and her willingness to adapt to whatever situation she found herself in.

He could see her in his mind's eye as the eager

little girl planting her garden and could see further to January, the mother, working next to her child to plant that garden of learning once again. Her child. Their child. *Their child?* The one they would create as they became one in a union like nothing he'd ever experienced before? A baby, suckling at January's breast as Houston looked on in awe, wonder, and . . . love?

Houston stiffened on the bench as the scenario unfolded in his mind. He ran a shaking hand down his face and shook his head. He couldn't, shouldn't, *wouldn't* fall in love with January. It was so damn wrong, it was pathetic. He had nothing to offer her but a middle-class home, in a middle-class suburb, surrounded by middle-class people.

No. No way. He wouldn't give full reign to the shadowy emotions he was registering that he was now pushing back, keeping simmering below the surface of his mind, not examining them too closely. He wouldn't listen to the voice of his heart and hear the message that he refused to heed. He leaned forward, resting his elbows on his knees and making a steeple of his fingers. Vivid pictures suddenly flitted before his eyes like a movie, beginning two months before with the minute he had seen January at the institute. He ran his finger over the bridge of his nose, a small smile tugging at his lips, then fading as he relived the weeks in Chicago when she'd never been far from his mind.

Scene by scene the events unfolded, ending with him envisioning January at that very moment asleep upstairs in the four-poster bed. Heat churned low in his body as his mind went past reality, seeing her lift her arms to him in a welcoming gesture; a soft, sensuous smile on her face.

Houston dragged his mind from the enticing scene, then glanced quickly around the room with the irrational thought that the fishermen had caught a glimpse of the intimate scenario. No one was paying any attention to him, and he redirected his attention to the fire.

What if there was a way, somehow, to make their worlds mesh, to reach a compromise, find a middle ground?

Whoa, Houston told himself. He was definitely getting crazy. There he sat, ready to slay the dragons of differences and carry his lady off into the night. Swell. Now he was a knight in shining armor instead of a ship's captain. Enough was enough. This nonsense was going to stop.

Houston glanced at his watch again, then got to his feet. January must be asleep by now, he decided. Upstairs, he stood outside his and January's door, then, feeling like a super sleuth, pressed his ear to the wooden panel. All was quiet. He inserted the key in the lock, turned it, then the knob, with infinite gentleness and slipped inside, closing the door behind him with a quiet click.

Darkness.

He couldn't see anything. It was like walking in an inkwell. The four-poster bed and January were over there someplace. The chairs he was going to push together and sleep on were somewhere to his left.

He moved forward.

A moment later, disaster struck.

He thudded against something that caught him at mid-thigh. In one smooth, reflex-filled motion he reached down, grabbed the offending object, and lifted it up and away with ease, despite its bulky weight. In the next instant, as he set it down away from him, he heard a splat, then a gasp, then . . .

A wild something catapulted off the floor and flung itself at him.

"Hi-yaa!" it shrieked, and landed against him.

The force and surprise of the impact caught Houston off guard, and he toppled backward, instinctively wrapping his arms around the creature attached to his body as he landed with an audible *oomph*, flat on his back on the floor.

"Let me go! Let me go! Let me go!" his attacker yelled.

"January?" Houston said, amazed there was any air left in his body.

"Let me— Houston?"

"Who in the hell did you think it was?" he said. Holy Toledo! His mind raced. She was stretched out along the length of him, his arms were wrapped around soft material that covered the oh, so feminine curves of her body. Her warm, sweet breath was feathering against his lips, and she smelled like wildflowers. He wasn't going to move for the next thirty years.

"You scared me to death, Houston Tyler."

"You were supposed to be in the bed."

"I was being a nice person by sleeping on the chairs. I certainly didn't expect to be attacked."

"I didn't attack you. *You* attacked *me*. What does 'Hi-yaa' mean?"

January laughed, causing her body to wiggle enticingly against his. Houston decided a man could die from such sweet torture, and it would be a hell of a fine way to go.

"I don't know what it means," January said. "I

heard it in a movie once." Oh, she thought, he felt so good, so strong, and she fit along his body like a spoon in a spoon rest. Her arms were resting on his chest, and she could just barely see the outline of his rugged features inches away. Houston was much more comfortable to lie on than those chairs. "I didn't hurt you, did I?"

"No. You just gave me a heart attack, that's all. I suppose I should let you get off me."

"I suppose," she said. Such heat. Such incredible heat was weaving from him into her, causing desire to swirl unchecked throughout her. Her breasts grew heavy, their fullness crushed to Houston's chest. She should move . . . she should. But he felt so good and smelled go good, and the wondrous sensations running rampant within her were just so good.

Heaven, Houston thought. Hot heaven thrumming through him with a burning heat. One kiss. Just one. Then he'd let her go.

"January," he murmured. He slid his hand to the nape of her neck, inched his long fingers into her silken curls, and urged her to dip her head to meet his lips.

Oh, thank goodness, she thought. He was going to kiss her.

She lowered her head, parted her lips, and met his mouth.

"Mmm," she said.

"Mmm," he echoed.

The kiss was incredible. Tongues sought and found each other as their mouths moved in a matching, hungry rhythm. Houston slid his other hand slowly down January's back, then over the slope of her buttocks to press her to him. His manhood strained against the zipper of his jeans as he nestled her to the heat, the want in the cradle of his hips.

Oh, how she wanted him, January thought, wanted to be one with him. He wanted her, too, she could feel it. She could feel the surge of his body beneath her; full, pressing against her, promising so much, so very much. Oh, Houston. Tonight could be theirs if he didn't turn her away again. She'd die, just die, if he rejected her.

Biological urges, Houston thought hazily. He had to remember that. He had to remember that it was only . . . "Biological urges," he murmured close to January's lips.

January came back from the rosy place she'd drifted to with a thud. "What? Oh, forget it, don't say it again." She wiggled off him, ignoring his groan, and got to her feet. "I'm going to bed"—she drew a steadying breath—"*in* the bed, Mr. Tyler. Good night." She paused. "Where's the bed?"

Houston struggled to his feet. "Why are you all in a snit?"

"I'm not," she said tightly, "in a snit. I would simply like to get some sleep." He hadn't rejected her, she told herself frantically. Not exactly. Just . . . sort of. He would have made love to her; she was nearly positive of that. But then he'd said those gruesome two words of his and ruined everything. Was she angry? Hurt? Mentally demolished? Oh, never mind. She was too tired to attempt to figure it all out. "Houston, where in heaven's name is the bed?"

"It's over there somewhere." He took her hand. "Come on. We'll find it eventually."

January laughed in spite of herself. "Or fall out the window."

They inched their way forward in the darkness until they thudded against the bed.

"Victory," Houston said.

"Houston, you can't possibly sleep on those chairs. I hardly fit on them. We'll have to share the bed." Was she nuts?

"That's not such a hot idea, January," he said. Bad choice of words, very bad.

"Don't be silly. We're mature adults. You stay on your side, I'll stay on mine." She crawled across the bed to the far side, pulled the blankets up to her chin, and closed her eyes. " 'Night."

"Yeah, good night," he said gruffly.

"It certainly is fortunate that we're only dealing in biological urges here, isn't it?" January asked pleasantly. "I mean, they're just so easily controlled due to the fact that there aren't any emotions involved." She yawned. "So sleepy." She flopped over onto her stomach and forced herself to breathe deeply and steadily.

Houston mumbled a few colorful expletives under his breath, stripped down to his underwear, and got into the bed, staying as close as possible to the edge. He tossed and turned restlessly for the next hour before drifting off into a light slumber.

On the other side of the bed, January was smiling.

Five

July 4

January slowly opened her eyes, allowing the delicious haze of sleep to fade at its leisure. She stretched, yawned, turned her head, then smiled. Houston.

She propped herself on one elbow and gazed at him, a frisson of heat sweeping through her as she replayed in her mind the exquisite sensations of their kiss the night before while she'd been stretched out along his rugged length. When she finally managed to fall asleep, she had dreamed of him making love to her.

She had never spent an entire night in a bed with a man, awakened by his side. Even though she and Houston hadn't actually made love, there was something special, so very intimate, about having him there so close, next to her.

Houston was on his stomach, the blankets to his

waist, revealing the bronzed, muscled beauty of his back, shoulders, and arms. His features were relaxed, his lips slightly parted, and January resisted the urge to trace her fingertip over those pleasure-giving lips, then brush back his thick, tousled auburn hair, which had tumbled onto his forehead.

So magnificent, she thought dreamily, then smiled. It was July Fourth. The Fourth of July, Independence Day. And she, January St. John, was questioning her desire to be the independent woman she had been for so long. Oh, she still wished to be a total woman within herself, but independent to the point of needing no one of importance in her life? No, maybe not. Did she want to be half of a whole, a partner and best friend, the wife of Houston Tyler? Did she want to stay by his side, have his children, grow old with him, and not part until death? Did she want it all? Was she in love with Houston?

January sank back against the pillow and stared at the ceiling. How was she to know? And if it was true, how was it all going to happen? What magic wand could she wave to make Houston declare his undying love for her, then in the next breath say to her that the differences in their worlds were unimportant and presented no obstacles to block the entrance to their Yellow Brick Road? A fairy godmother would help immensely, but Cinderella had cornered the market on the supply.

No, January decided, there were no magic potions or little elves to solve the dilemma. Time was the key. And heaven knew, she had come to cherish every moment of time spent with Houston.

She gasped as a large hand slid across the soft material of the nightie covering her stomach, and she turned her head again to gaze into warm brown eyes.

"Hello," she said, smiling.

"Hello, yourself," Houston said, his voice gruff with sleep. "You're nice to wake up to."

"So are you."

Their gazes held in a long, long moment. Fingers of heated desire crept throughout January, showing themselves in a warm flush on her cheeks. Houston felt his manhood stir with his desire for the woman who was so enticingly close to him. With a groan he forced his gaze from January's and rolled onto his back, shoving his hands beneath his head.

"Do you suppose," he said, "that life was simpler back in the days of tall ships and sea captains? Or maybe in the days of knights in shining armor?"

"I doubt it," January said. "Every era in history had its problems to overcome. But they did, you know, overcome their problems, go after their hopes and dreams."

"Yeah, I suppose."

"Everyone should have dreams, Houston."

"I agree. And right now I'm dreaming of breakfast. Come, fair maiden, we are about to shower, dress, and eat. I need food!"

Houston flipped the blankets off her, waved her from the bed, then pointed to the shower. She dashed across the floor as Houston watched, their laughter bouncing off the walls and filling the room to overflowing.

The mood was set.

It was a glorious day. A warm, sunny, exciting

day. It was a day of smiles and laughter, stolen kisses at every opportunity, and taking part in an old-fashioned celebration of the Fourth of July.

Instead of a conventional parade, the patriotic display was a seemingly endless stream of boats of every shape and size passing on the water. They tooted horns, waved flags, and the throng on the shore cheered their approval.

There were games for all ages, folk dancing, rows of tables groaning under the weight of delicious food. Houston entered a log-splitting contest and won the first-place blue ribbon. January entered the bean-bag toss and lost when hers landed in a huge bowl of potato salad.

"I'm surprised at you," Houston said, grinning at her. "Your aim sure wasn't off the mark when your fist connected with my nose."

January glared at him.

In the afternoon, the storyteller arrived and the children ran after him to a grassy slope to hear him spin his tales. January plopped down on the grass and listened, a look of spellbound rapture on her face. Houston gazed only at January, his heart doing a strange tap dance.

Later the homemade crafts were brought out for sale; jellies, jams, aprons, quilts, jewelry created from shells, centerpieces from driftwood. There were sunbonnets and fishing flies, knitted mittens and scarves, delicate crocheted tablecloths.

Hand in hand, January and Houston strolled from one display to the next, marveling at the beauty of the work.

"Oh, Houston, look," January said. "That quilt is exquisite. There must be a million tiny stitches in it. And the colors . . . like a softly muted rainbow. See how those two circles intertwine?"

"It's a wedding quilt," the woman behind the table said. "Those circles are wedding rings connected together, never to be separated again."

"Oh," January said, leaning closer to it. "It's beautiful."

"Back in my grandmother's day," the woman went on, "every bride received a wedding quilt. It was a very important tradition. During the reception, after the ceremony, the quilt was placed on the bride and groom's bed and would be there when they arrived in their room later for their wedding night. Through the years it was washed, mended, might even become threadbare, but it remained on the bed until one of them died."

"Then what?" Houston asked.

"It was wrapped in tissue and put away. The folklore of the quilt said that as it was folded, the memories of the happy years were guarded inside and never could be lost."

"I like that story," Houston said, nodding. "That's nice, really nice. I'll take that quilt. Could you wrap it up for me?"

"Certainly," the woman said. "I hope it brings you and your wife"—she smiled at January—"many years of happiness."

January looked up quickly at Houston, but he didn't meet her gaze as he paid for the quilt, then made arrangements for the bulky package to be delivered to the inn.

A wedding quilt? January's mind echoed. For Houston and his wife? The wife he intended to find in

July? The woman he'd search for once he'd dusted January out of his mind? Oh, how depressing.

"All set?" Houston said when he'd finished his transaction. "How about something cool to drink?"

"Sure," January said, pushing aside her racing thoughts. "It's amazingly warm considering what it was like yesterday."

"Yep," he said, nodding. "There's some lemonade over there."

They got their drinks, then walked down to the beach to sit on the sand.

"I like that quilt," Houston said, sliding January a quick glance. "Traditions are nice, have a sense of permanence, don't you think? We need continuity in our society of disposable items."

"I agree. Not all men, however, would admit to being sentimental."

"I'm a sentimental guy," he said, grinning. "When you're as big as I am, you can be anything you want to, and no one is in a hurry to hassle you about it. If I feel like singing along with the piped-in Christmas carols in shopping centers at the holidays, I just do it. Very sentimental, that's me. Did you like the quilt?"

"It's lovely," January said softly, staring into her drink.

Why had he bought that quilt? Houston asked himself. And why was it suddenly important to him that January liked it and the tradition that went along with it? It was a wedding quilt, for Pete's sake.

A shout went up, saying that dinner was served, and enormous quantities of food were once more consumed. As darkness fell, everyone hurried to find a place on the beach as a large barge chugged into view. Then, with the appropriate oohs and aahs, the crowd watched the spectacle of fireworks explode into the sky in vibrant colors.

January sat close to Houston's side, his arm snugly around her shoulders. He kissed her on the temple and she smiled, savoring the peace and joy that filled her. Savoring the feel, aroma, and heat of Houston.

The day drew to a close. Sleepy children were carried from the beach, farewells were exchanged, and people slowly dispersed, seeming reluctant to end the hours of fun.

January and Houston walked back to the inn chatting comfortably about the many activities they'd shared. In their room, their glance fell on the wrapped quilt, which had been placed on one of the chairs, but neither of them mentioned it.

Houston shoved his hands into his pockets and looked at January. "I'm going to go back downstairs for a while." He cleared his throat. "I want you, January, you know that. But . . . well, things are complicated enough without . . . do you understand?"

She smiled. "Yes, I understand."

"Good. Okay." He hurried to the door. "Sleep well."

January stood in the quiet room, her smile firmly in place. Oh, yes, she understood, she thought. Houston wasn't listening to his own words. Things were complicated enough? Didn't he see, didn't he realize, that emotions were now intertwined with his ever-famous biological urges? What all those emotions were, she wasn't sure, but they were there. Oh, my, yes, they were there.

"Good night, Houston," she whispered.

July 5

Early the next morning, January and Houston were deposited on the island that had been their original destination. The owner of the small boat settled back with a newspaper and told them to take all the time they needed.

"I'll be right here when you get back," the man said. "Saves me from having to help the wife weed the garden. That woman can find a chore a minute for me to do. Don't rush, folks."

January and Houston laughed, then set off, following a simply drawn map that January had.

"Have you seen this house?" Houston said as they walked through the thick grass.

"No, I had nothing to do with this. The island was purchased by St. John Enterprises as a possible site for a resort. The man in charge of the project is down with the flu, so here I am. The decision to be made is whether or not to remodel what's here, or to tear it down and start over. I didn't read the official report. For all I know, it's nothing more than a ramshackle mess."

It wasn't.

As the huge structure came into view, their eyes widened and their steps quickened. They stopped in front and stared.

"Oh, Houston," January said, "can you believe this? It looks like an old Southern plantation house, complete with pillars and veranda. I expect Scarlett O'Hara to come out the front door at any moment. I certainly didn't anticipate anything like this off the coast of Maine, for goodness sake. It's beautiful, absolutely beautiful."

When Houston didn't reply, January looked up at

him. His gaze was sweeping over the entire two-story house, his brown eyes sparkling with excitement. There was an expression of awe on his face, which brought a soft smile to January's lips.

"*Bee-yoo-tee-ful*," Houston said. "Lord, I hope it's structurally sound. I hate the thought of tearing this down. Cancel the sea captain and the knight. I am now, madam"—he covered his heart with his hand—"a fine Southern gentleman. Come, my little magnolia, and we shall explore our mansion. Y'all are the fairest belle in the land of Dixie, and I'm the master of this plantation."

"Got it," January said, laughing. "I mean, I'd be honored, sir, to accompany y'all into . . . we have to name it, Houston. All the old homes in the South had names."

Houston bowed deeply, then swept his arm in the direction of the house. "Welcome to January Hall."

January stood on tiptoe, flung her arms around Houston's neck, and kissed him full on the lips. "You named it after me?"

"Damn right," he said, then brought his mouth down hard onto hers.

Houston gathered January close to his body as the kiss intensified, and she answered the demands of his lips and tongue. Their breathing was labored when he finally released her.

"Y'all are one . . ." Houston began, then took a deep breath. ". . . potent magnolia."

"Why, sir," she said, batting her eyelashes at him, "whatever do y'all mean?"

"I mean, madam," he said, merriment dancing in his eyes, "that you are one helluva kisser."

"You bet I am, buster," she said, whopping him

on the arm. Houston laughed in delight. "Let's go inside, Houston. I can hardly wait to see what it looks like. Oh, heavens, I wonder if it has one of those sweeping staircases? If it does, will you carry me up like Rhett did to Scarlett?"

"Oh, my aching back," Houston moaned.

January then stomped up the front steps, Houston following close behind.

January dug in the pocket of her jeans for a key. "I want to be carried up the stairs like Scarlett."

"I can't do it. My war injury, you know."

"What war?"

"The Civil War, of course. Open the door."

January rolled her eyes heavenward, then unlocked the door and pushed it open. They stepped inside.

"Oh . . . my," she said. "Oh, my goodness."

There was, indeed, a wide sweeping staircase off to the right, and above them in the entryway was an enormous chandelier that tinkled like wind chimes in the breeze from the open door. They walked slowly forward.

"Incredible," Houston said. His glance fell on the stairs. "You win. That staircase is calling my name." He turned, flipped January over his shoulder, and circled her legs with his arm. "Here we go, Scarlett."

"Houston!" she yelled. "This isn't how Rhett did it. I'm not supposed to be hauled up the stairs like a sack of potatoes!"

"Picky, picky, picky," he said, then went to the stairs. He sprinted up, two at a time.

"Oh-h-h!" January hollered.

At the top of the stairs Houston set her on her feet. He wasn't even breathing heavily, while she stood gasping.

"What's your problem?" he asked.

"The blood ran to my head, and you bounced all the air out of my body."

"There's no pleasing some people. I carried you up the stairs, didn't I?"

"Hmm," she said, glaring at him.

"Okay, let's get serious here. You can poke around to your heart's content while I check out the plumbing, wiring, see if there are any nasty little termites in residence."

"All right," she said. "Oh, look at all the doors. It's like Christmas, with a surprise behind every one." She started off down the hall.

Houston watched her for a long moment until she disappeared into the first room. He turned and went slowly down the stairs.

Amazing, he thought. January was amazing. Surely she'd been in some of the biggest, fanciest homes in the country, even the world. Yet her eyes were glowing with excitement over this empty, dusty place. She had a gift for appreciating to the fullest the moment she was in, cherishing all that it offered. But this house, like the inn, wasn't quite real, was a step removed from the world in which January functioned on a daily basis. They'd go to New York that afternoon, then he'd see, really see, January St. John.

In the meantime? he asked himself. He was Colonel Tyler of January Hall, inspecting his estate.

"Yes, suh, Colonel, suh," he said, saluting himself in a dusty mirror in the entryway. "You're cracking up, Tyler," he muttered, then strode down the hall.

Two hours later when Houston found January,

she was exploring what had been the library in the house. His announcement that the structure was sound brought a shout of delight from her. She flung herself into Houston's arms and insisted on giving him a tour of the twelve bedrooms, eight bathrooms, the living room, the kitchen, and on and on. Houston didn't have the heart to tell her that he'd seen them all and allowed himself to be dragged along for the tour.

It was going to be a wonderful vacation resort, January had chattered, and Houston was soon caught up in her enthusiasm, suggesting that the employees dress in costumes of the era of the plantation days in the South. He finally reminded her that they still had to fly to New York that day, and with a sigh January had agreed to head back to the boat, glancing often at the house as they walked away.

The owner of the boat was enjoying a nap when they arrived. When they woke him, he said they sure hadn't stayed long, and he'd still have to do chores for his wife. Back at the inn, January and Houston showered and changed, Houston's slacks and sport coat having been pressed by the wife of the owner of the inn. They contacted Terry, said they were on their way, and set off in the pickup truck. The wrapped quilt Houston had purchased lay between them on the seat.

As the plane winged its way through the heavens, Houston looked out the window. Well, he mused, back to reality. Gone were the sea captain, the knight in shining armor, the Southern colonel. He was simply Houston Tyler, construction worker, blue-collar, middle-class.

But he was not, he knew, the same man who had gotten on that plane two days before. Then his mission had been clear: To free his mind of the hold that January had over him. It had been as simple as that. But now? Now emotions were churning within him, demanding attention. Emotions centered on January St. John and what was happening between them. Was he in love with her? Dammit, where did a man find the answer to a question like that? Was the aching need and want of her more than just biological urges? And if he really did love her, was there any hope that they could find a middle ground between their worlds?

Houston turned to look at January, who had her nose buried in a magazine. She was wearing white linen slacks and a blue silk blouse; as usual, her shoes were dumped onto the floor. He resisted the urge to weave his fingers through her silken curls and bring her mouth to his for a searing kiss. He wanted to carry her to the small bedroom in the rear of the plane and make love to her, right then and there.

Right, Houston's mind taunted. The closer they got to New York, the bigger the knot in his gut grew. Ah, damn, what was he going to do? He was so confused, and the bottom line was, what did he have, really have, to offer January except maybe, just maybe, his love and a homemade wedding quilt? Beyond that? Nothing. Nothing at all.

"Nope," January said.

"What?" Houston said, having the irrational thought that she'd read his mind.

"This decorating magazine didn't have what I was looking for," she said, placing it on a table. "It's all contemporary groupings. I was thinking, Houston, that each room of January Hall could be done in a different color and mood. You know, the gold room, the blue room, the pink room. Or maybe name the rooms after flowers. How's that? The guest would call and say, 'I'd like to reserve the Magnolia Room.' "

Houston laughed. "If it were me, I'd feel like an idiot."

She frowned. "Oh."

"You're really excited about that place, aren't you?"

"Oh, yes," she said. "I can see it all so clearly in my mind when it's decorated and ready for visitors. I was even impressed with how it looked today."

"It was something, all right. The outside needs painting, and it would have to be landscaped, but the inside just needs a good cleaning, and whatever decorating you plan on doing. If you hustled, I imagine you could have it staffed and furnished in time to advertise for the tourist season next summer. I think you'd have to advertise by Christmas, but I'm no expert on the subject."

"Well, I'm just dreaming, anyway," January said. "It's not my project."

"So?" Houston shrugged. "Tell whoever is in charge that you're taking over."

"I can't do that."

"Why not? The island and the house belong to St. John Enterprises, and you're January St. John. What's the problem?"

"I have assigned duties that keep me very busy. Besides, my mother doesn't allow me to abuse my position with the company. After I write my report and turn it in I have to concentrate on my own work. Requests for grants will be flooding in for the fall season. I'll wade through them, actually go see some of the research projects for myself, then make my decisions."

"Sounds rather boring."

"It's challenging. I really enjoy it. But . . . never mind."

"But what?"

"But at the moment all I can think about is January Hall. I'll just have to push it from my mind."

"Get it out of your system," Houston said gruffly. He turned to look out the window again. "Right. Just get a big broom and sweep away all that garbage."

"Houston, what's wrong? You seem angry about something."

"No," he said, meeting her gaze again, "I'm not angry." He was confused as hell, dammit. "I'm fine." He got to his feet and roamed around the cabin.

Something was wrong, January thought, watching him. Houston was growing more tense by the moment; she could feel it. He was like a caged lion waiting to break free of his restraints. Was he tired of the long hours he'd been forced to be in her company? Hours that had included tender moments and shared kisses? She'd kill him! He wouldn't dare be tired of her. He just wouldn't dare. Would he?

"Houston, I wish you'd tell me what has brought on this gloomy mood of yours. I, for one, had a marvelous time in Maine. We shared . . . well, you know what we shared."

Houston stopped in front of her, leaned over and

gripped the arms of the chair, and spoke close to her lips, a muscle jumping along his jaw.

"Yes," he said, his voice low, ominously low, "I know what we shared. The question is, now what? Thanks for the good time, Houston? You're a dynamite kisser, Houston, but get out of my face? I have grants to grant, or whatever the hell you do, so shuffle off to Buffalo, Houston?"

"What on earth is the matter with you?" January said, her voice rising. "This whole thing was just as much your cockamamie idea as mine, remember? We were supposed to be staying alert, not succumbing. Well, guess what? I succumbed. So sue me."

Houston suddenly grinned. "You didn't dust me off?"

"No. Now go away. You've got me pinned in this chair like a trapped mouse. Shoo."

"Shoo?"

"Yes, shoo. No, wait. As long as we're reporting in, what's the status of your system, Mr. Tyler?" January asked, glaring at him. Oh, Houston, please, please, please? He hadn't left Maine with an empty heart, had he? Ready to fill it up with the woman he'd set out to find? The ever-famous Miss July? "Well?"

"You want a report?" Houston asked slowly.

"Fair is fair, tit for tat. Since I have admitted that this trip did not solve anything for me, I feel I have the right to know where you stand on the subject at this point in time." Not bad. Nice stuffy little spiel.

"My, my," Houston said, still smiling, "what a stuffy little spiel."

January narrowed her eyes. "You're beginning to

get on my nerves, Houston Tyler. Shoo. I don't like being trapped in this chair."

"This chair is bothering you? Well, now, my little magnolia, I'll just take care of that for you in a jiffy."

"What do you plan . . . oh!" she said with a gasp. She was suddenly airborne as Houston scooped her out of the chair, one arm under her knees, the other nestled beneath her breasts. He held her tightly to his chest, and she stared at him with startled gray eyes. "Oh," she repeated weakly.

"Now for my report."

"Houston, put me down."

"No."

"Whatever," she said, examining her fingernails. "If you want to stand there straining your Civil War injury, who am I to argue with you?"

"Precisely." He paused. "Do you want to hear my report or not?"

No! her mind screamed. "I suppose," she said. Had she sounded bored? She was trying for bored, but she had a feeling it had been a pretty shaky bored. "Carry on."

"Look at me."

"No."

"Look . . . at . . . me."

"Lord, you're crabby," she said, meeting his gaze. "Do you know how dumb you appear, Mr. Tyler, standing in the middle of an airplane holding a woman in your arms as though you think it will help the plane fly higher or something?"

Houston shifted her slightly in his arms so that his thumb could stroke the nipple of one of her breasts. The bud became taut beneath the silk of her blouse and the wispy material of her bra.

"Dumb, huh?" he said, his voice deep and rumbly. "Is that a fact?"

"Yep."

He shifted her again, her breast now cupped in his palm as his thumb got busier. January swallowed heavily.

"Really dumb?" Houston asked in a husky whisper.

Oh, Lordy, she was dying, January thought, swallowing another nearly hysterical giggle. Heated desire was pulsing throughout her, Houston was driving her crazy with the want of him, and he knew it, the louse.

"Sir," she said stiffly, "may I please have your report?" Then he could get to the good stuff, like tearing off her clothes and ravishing her body. Oh, January, for shame.

"Yes, ma'am. Certainly, ma'am. My brain"—Houston brushed his lips over hers—"is consumed by thoughts of you." He outlined her lips with the tip of his tongue. January shivered. "I, too"—he sucked her lower lip—"have succumbed."

January purred. "Oh, thank heavens," she said, wrapping her arms around his neck.

"Then there's my body. Oh, my poor body," he went on. He trailed nibbling kisses down her throat. "I want you, January St. John," he murmured. "But then, you know that, don't you?"

"Oh, I know, I know. I want you, too, Houston. I—"

"Buckle up, folks," Terry said over the intercom. "I'm on the approach to Kennedy."

Houston rolled his eyes to the heavens. "I used to like that guy."

"Houston?" January said softly. "Were you serious?"

"Yeah," he said quietly. "Yeah, I think about you all the time. We're going to have to talk, January. Later."

He claimed her mouth in a hard kiss, then deposited her back in the chair. He hunkered down in front of her and reached for her seat belt, his knuckles brushing against her stomach as he fastened it. January ran her fingertip lightly over his lips. Houston lifted his head to look at her, their eyes meeting for a long, quiet moment.

"You'd better buckle up," January finally said, a breathless quality to her voice.

"January, I . . . yeah," he said, then moved to his chair and snapped the belt in place. He looked out the window and saw the first streaks of the summer sunset, sending an eerie glow over the sprawling city below. He wanted to leap to his feet, go tell Terry to turn the plane around, and take January and Houston back. Take them back to January Hall on the beautiful little island. They could fix the house up together, make it into a fantastic resort. He did not want to go back to the real world.

"Houston?"

"Yeah?" he said, snapping his head around to look at January.

"I never asked you if you'd stay at my apartment while you're in New York. Will you?"

He reached over and covered her hand with his on the arm of the chair. "There's nowhere else I'd want to be."

"My apartment is . . . well, it's . . . oh, darn it, Houston, it's across from Central Park, and it's big and fancy and cost a bundle, and you'll hate it, I know."

America's most popular, most compelling romance novels...

Here, at last...love stories that really involve you! Fresh, finely crafted novels with story lines so believable you'll feel you're actually living them! Characters you can relate to...exciting places to visit...unexpected plot twists...all in all, exciting romances that satisfy your mind and delight your heart.

EXAMINE 6 LOVESWEPT NOVELS FOR

15 Days FREE!

To introduce you to this fabulous service, you'll get six brand-new Loveswept releases not yet in the bookstores. These six exciting new titles are yours to examine for 15 days without obligation to buy. Keep them if you wish for just $12.50 plus postage and handling and any applicable sales tax.

☐ **YES,** please send me six new romances for a 15-day FREE examination. If I keep them, I will pay just $12.50 (that's six books for the price of five) plus postage and handling and any applicable sales tax and you will enter my name on your preferred customer list to receive all six new Loveswept novels published each month *before* they are released to the bookstores—always on the same 15-day free examination basis.

40311

Name_____

Address_____

City_____

State_____ Zip_____

My Guarantee: I am never required to buy any shipment unless I wish. I may preview each shipment for 15 days. If I don't want it, I simply return the shipment within 15 days and owe nothing for it.

R623

Get one full-length Loveswept FREE every month!
Now you can be sure you'll never, ever miss a single
Loveswept title by enrolling in our special reader's home
delivery service. A service that will bring you all six new
Loveswept romances each month for the price of five—and
deliver them to you before they appear in the bookstores!

Examine 6 Loveswept Novels for

15 days FREE!

(SEE OTHER SIDE FOR DETAILS)

Postage will be paid by addressee

Loveswept

Bantam Books
P.O. Box 985
Hicksville, NY 11802

BUSINESS REPLY MAIL

FIRST-CLASS MAIL   PERMIT NO. 2456   HICKSVILLE, NY

NO POSTAGE
NECESSARY
IF MAILED
IN THE
UNITED STATES

"Look, I—"

"I've lived there so long, I don't even think about it. I'm trying to see it fresh in my mind, through your eyes. It jumps up and down, and shouts 'Money!' at the top of its lungs."

Houston laughed. "That's a very talented apartment you have there. It does a vaudeville routine. Don't worry about it. I really didn't expect you to live in a tenement, you know."

"You're going to hate it, definitely hate it."

"January," he said, squeezing her hand, "if I were going to make love to you tonight, would it matter if it's in a bed that cost five thousand dollars, or one bought at a secondhand store? What's important here? What we might share, or the surroundings we're sharing it in?"

"What a lovely thing to say," she said softly. But did he believe it? she wondered. Really, really believe it?

Had he actually said all that? Houston asked himself. *He* was reassuring *her*? He was the one who didn't have a nickel to his name compared to her. But the point he had made was valid. His focus, his thoughts, his attention were centered on January, not on the quality and cost of the chair or sofa she might be sitting on. And making love? Hell, he could make love to her in a one-room shack with a bare light bulb hanging from the ceiling, and it would be a beautiful, incredibly beautiful, joining between a man and a woman.

"Houston?" January said, pulling him from his reverie.

"Yes?"

"Did you mean what you just said, really mean it?

When we're together tonight, are you positive it isn't going to make a difference that we're in an apartment across from Central Park?"

He sighed. "I meant it. But I have to remember that we're still up here in the clouds. In another few minutes we'll be back to the real world."

"I see," she said quietly.

"No, I'm the one who will see, January, and it's long overdue."

A silence fell as both January and Houston became lost in their own jumbled thoughts.

Six

Houston stood staring out the large window of January's apartment, seeing the dancing lights of the bustling city. He turned slowly to survey the living room, marveling yet again at the welcoming warmth it exuded despite its size.

This was January's home. He'd been prepared to be overwhelmed by the opulence he knew he would find. But it hadn't happened. Yes, it was big, and yes, it was obviously furnished with the finest furniture available, but January's touch had created a homey atmosphere.

When January had kicked off her shoes the moment they had entered, he'd smiled in delight and felt the tension begin to ebb from his tightly coiled muscles. Dinner had been a simple affair of omelets, toast, and coffee, then January had waved him out of the kitchen while she loaded the dishwasher. Now he stood once again in her living room, feeling remarkably like he belonged.

"All done," January said. "I'll call in an order for groceries tomorrow." She crossed the room to stand in front of him. "You look awfully serious. Is something wrong? If you absolutely hate this apartment, don't tell me. I did warn you, you know."

Houston drew her into the circle of his arms. "I've discovered I really like this place. I'm comfortable, and I didn't expect to be."

"You do? You like it? Really?"

"Really," he said, lowering his lips toward hers. "We're smack-dab in the middle of reality and doing fine."

"Oh, Houston."

He claimed her mouth with an intensity that both shocked and pleased her, and she answered the demands of his lips and tongue in total abandon. He gathered her close, his hands roaming restlessly over her back. January's knees began to buckle.

He was already at the edge of his control, Houston realized hazily. The days and nights spent with January had taken their toll. His need for her was beyond anything he'd ever known.

"Houston, please," January whispered.

Ah, damn, he thought wildly, those words again. But this time, *this time* he was going to find out exactly what she meant.

"Please what?" he said, his voice raspy with passion. "I have to know, January. Are you asking me to stop?"

Was he insane? She nearly shouted. "Houston, I want you," she said, hearing the breathlessness in her voice. "I want to make love with you."

"Are you sure?" he said. "You have to be. Please,

January, this is important. How can we be certain that it isn't just . . ."

"Biological urges," she finished for him. "Houston, I want you, I'm very sure, and I know it's important. I don't know what else to say, except please, please, Houston, make love with me."

With a groan he captured her head in his hands and brought her lips to his for a hard, searing kiss. When he released her, he swung her up into his arms, one arm beneath her knees, the other under her breasts. He held her tightly to him as though afraid she would float away as he crossed the room and went down the hall to the master bedroom. He set her on her feet next to the big bed, snapped on the lamp on the nightstand, and in the rosy glow of light, their eyes met. Brown eyes, gray eyes, smoky with desire, sending and receiving the same message of desire, and erasing any doubts that may have lingered.

In unspoken agreement, in acknowledgment of their fiery need, they moved to a set of easy chairs and removed their clothes, tossing them haphazardly on the velvet chairs. At the exact same moment they turned toward each other . . . then stopped.

Their gazes traveled over each other, as though each were alone, viewing a precious statue, a gift meant only for them. What they saw would be theirs to have, totally, completely. Waves of sensuality seemed to weave between them as the silken threads tugged at senses and ignited passions further.

"You are exquisite," Houston said, his voice gritty.

"You take my breath away," January said softly.

Their eyes met again, then Houston lifted his hand and extended it palm-up to January.

Neither spoke, nor hardly breathed. It was the turning point, a moment like no other. Houston's simple gesture spoke volumes, and January's hand was trembling as she placed it in his. His fingers curled around hers as though sealing a bond of trust.

He closed the distance between them and gathered her close to his body, holding her, just holding her, as though she were made of the most delicate crystal.

January's eyes misted with tears at the sheer beauty of the quiet moment. They were naked in each other's arms, bare, vulnerable, and she felt more cherished, protected, and feminine than she had in her entire life.

Houston closed his eyes for a moment as he fought for control. He savored the feel of January's soft body against his heated skin and inhaled her aroma. The fear of hurting her shuddered through his mind, and he gritted his teeth, vowing to go slow, to be certain she had all the time she needed to be ready for what he would bring to her.

He lifted her onto the cool sheets, then moved next to her. Their eyes met, their lips met, their tongues met.

Houston rested on one arm, his other hand trailing down January's throat, then on to one breast, his thumb stroking the nipple to a taut bud. He went lower, to the flat plane of her stomach, then to the dark curls that guarded her femininity. He thrust his tongue deeper into her mouth as his fingers inched onward.

Desire swept through January, her body seeming

to hum with tingling need. A driving cadence deep inside her was matched by the rhythm of Houston's tongue, and then—oh, merciful heaven—then by his fingers that were discovering all that she was. His manhood was heavy against her hip; hot, throbbing, filled with sensual promise. And she wanted him. Now.

Houston drew his mouth from hers to take a ragged breath.

"Houston, come to me," she pleaded. "Oh, I want you so much."

"I will," he said, his voice sounding strange to his own ears. "Soon. I don't want to hurt you. I have to be sure you're ready for me. Soon, January."

Then, where his hand had journeyed, his lips followed. He drew the bud of one breast deep into his mouth, suckling, pulling, until January was arching her back to give him more, tangling her fingers into his thick hair to press his mouth harder onto her soft flesh. He moved to the other breast, and she nearly sobbed with the ecstasy of the sweet foray. He skimmed his lips to her stomach, then beyond.

"Houston! Oh, dear heaven, please."

"Yes," he said hoarsely. "Yes, now. Oh, Lord, you want me, your body is so ready for me. Ah, January."

He moved over her, resting on his forearms, then gazed directly into her eyes. He entered her slowly, watching her face. Her eyes widened for a moment at the sheer size and power of him, then a soft smile formed on her lips.

"Oh, yes, Houston."

"It's all for you," he said, his muscles trembling from forced restraint. "Easy. Slow and easy. I won't hurt you. You're so small, so tight. You feel so damn good."

January shifted her hips slightly, and he groaned as he went deeper into her. Her moist heat closed around him, receiving him, welcoming him. Slowly, slowly, and she took all that he was.

He kissed her, then began to move within her. Slowly.

"Yes," she said, playing her hands on his moist, muscled back. "Oh, yes." She wrapped her legs around his powerful thighs and urged him on, arching her back to bring him closer yet.

Houston increased the tempo. January matched it. Restraint was forgotten. The cadence was pounding, perfect. Sensations gathered like a tempest; swirling, pulsing, heated. Glorious.

"Houston!" January gasped, gripping his shoulders. "Yes!"

Spasms swept through January. Spasms of ecstasy, and a moment later Houston drove one last time deep, so deep, within her, then stiffened, his head thrown back as his life's force pulsed within her. He groaned in pleasure, then in a smooth motion rolled over, taking her with him, their bodies still one entity.

January rested her head on his chest, unable to speak, feeling his heart gradually return to a normal, steady beat, as did her own.

"Oh, Houston," she said finally.

That was all, just "Oh, Houston," and he felt a tightening in his throat from the joy that filled him. And then he knew. He was in love with January St. John. The confusion within him quieted, and he refused to embrace any thoughts of the problems still to be solved. He wished only to savor the moment, the knowledge that he loved her. Loved his January. In July.

"Unbelievable," he said.

"Magnificent."

January was talking about their lovemaking, he realized. Should he tell her that he loved her? No, not now. Not yet. He had to get used to the idea first. He was in love!

"Houston, are you there?"

"I didn't hurt you, did I? I'm so big and—"

"I know," she said, a wistful tone to her voice.

He chuckled, causing her head to bounce on his chest. "I guess I didn't hurt you."

"Mmm. No."

"Excuse me," he said, "but are you planning on sleeping on top of me for the rest of the night?"

"I'm considering it," she said dreamily. "I never knew that muscles could be so comfy." She wiggled a bit, as though settling into a favorite position.

Houston groaned. "Don't do that, or your sleep is going to be postponed."

She wiggled again.

"January!"

Slowly, sensuously, she slid her hands down his chest as she leveled herself upward, straddling his hips as his manhood surged within her. Her gaze lingered on the sight of their joined bodies, then she looked into his eyes. Sweat dotted his brow.

"Do I feel good, Houston?" she whispered. "Do you like this? I think it's wonderful." She rotated her hips in a slow circle.

"Lord," he said, gritting his teeth, "I'm going to explode. January, what if I hurt you? Can you feel what you're doing to me? I can't . . . hold back . . . any longer."

"Help me, Houston. Now, now."

With a strangled moan he gripped her hips and lifted her slightly, rising to meet her. They rode the pounding waves of passion as one. Together. Higher. They called to each other, their bodies slick with perspiration as the tempo increased and the spiraling tension grew. January closed her eyes as her summit was reached, then Houston rolled her over onto her back and shuddered within her as he joined her in the place where she had gone. He collapsed against her in total exhaustion but stayed only a moment before moving his weight off her, then pulled her to his side.

"Lord," he said, gasping for breath. "I don't know what to say to you. That was . . . it really was."

"Mmm, yes."

He reached for the blankets, then turned out the light.

"Are you all right?" he asked, his lips resting lightly on her forehead.

"I'm sensational," she murmured.

He smiled. "That's no joke. You're really something, January St. John."

"No, I mean you made me feel . . . you know what I meant."

"*We're* sensational. Together."

"Mmm."

"Go to sleep," he said.

"Good night, Houston," she whispered.

"Good night," he said. *Sleep well, my love, my January. January in July,* he thought. Perfect.

And then they slept.

Hours later January woke with a start, feeling as though someone had called to her to bring her from her deep, dreamless sleep. She was nestled close to Houston in the darkness, and she savored the remembrance of the lovemaking they'd shared.

Then, in a message clearly delivered, she heard the voice of her heart.

She was in love with Houston Tyler.

The final question had been answered, and it was glorious. She loved him.

With a soft smile on her lips, she drifted back to sleep.

July 15

January looked up as Houston came striding into her office, deeply engrossed in an open folder he held in his hands. She watched as he closed the door, strode across the deep-piled carpeting, and sank into the leather chair behind the desk that had been brought into her office to give him room to work.

Unbelievable, January thought. There he was, Houston Tyler, in his faded jeans and knit shirt, sitting a few feet away from where she sat in her cranberry-colored linen suit and raw silk blouse. Houston needed a trim; his thick, auburn hair was beginning to curl over his ears and the collar of his shirt. She'd had a shampoo and shaping at an expensive salon only the day before. Houston smelled, she knew, like fresh soap and pure male, while she had a dab of hundred-dollar-an-ounce French perfume behind each ear and between her breasts.

Yes, there he sat in a plush office at St. John Enterprises, looking like a refugee from a construction site, and the unbelievable, absolutely incredible part was . . . he fit in!

January tapped the eraser end of her pencil against her chin and stared at the ceiling, recalling how she and Houston had returned from Maine to find St. John Enterprises in an uproar. They were, Sara St. John had explained, in the middle of a flu epidemic. It was amazing how many employees had fallen victim to the malady, and St. John Enterprises was short of personnel in every department. Sara had laughed, said that the stricken workers were convinced they should make out their wills, then she had shaken Houston's hand and asked him if he'd like a temporary job to help fill in where needed. Houston instantly agreed.

Two days later Houston had flown back to the island to supervise the painting of the outside of January Hall and to see to the clearing of the weeds to make the area ready for landscaping. He had also hired local help to clean the inside of the house from top to bottom.

Left behind in Manhattan, January had met with decorators, landscapers, and advertising people for hours each day, finally dragging herself home at night to fall across her bed in an exhausted heap.

But not too tired, she knew, to miss Houston. To reach for Houston in the night, only to find the expanse of bed next to her empty. The lovemaking

JANUARY IN JULY • 103

they had shared there had been exquisite. January had basked in Houston's attention, adored waking up in the morning nestled close to him and falling asleep in his arms at night.

They had had only two days before Houston had returned to Maine, and now he'd been back for two days. At her mother's urging, January had turned over her reports on January Hall to Houston to free January to do her own work on reviewing the requests for grants that were flooding in. Sara St. John, January realized, had instantly liked and respected Houston, as had those he came in contact with at St. John Enterprises.

And there he was, January mentally rambled, in one of the swankiest offices in Manhattan in his faded jeans, needing a haircut, and he looked so darn right amid the plush surroundings that it was ridiculous. No one, Sara included, questioned Houston's mode of dress or his need of a haircut. He was Houston, and they sensed, saw, and felt the integrity in his eyes and the firmness of his handshake. He had not been accepted to please January but had won their trust and admiration on his own merit.

And, oh, mercy, January thought, sighing inwardly, how she loved him.

She smiled at Houston where he sat with his head bent over the file. It was a dreamy smile, a woman-in-love smile, an everything-is-wonderful smile. But then the smile slowly faded and was replaced by a frown.

This wasn't real, she thought dismally. The life she and Houston had led since returning to New York was no closer to the norm than the days they'd spent together in Maine. St. John Enterprises was in a state of emergency, with top executives typing their own letters and messenger boys answering telephones. Slowly but surely, the flu victims were returning to work, but it would be a while before everyone was back in their proper places. January and Houston were putting in long, grueling days at the office, grabbing a quick dinner, then heading for her apartment where they made sweet, sensuous love before falling asleep.

But it wasn't real!

January glanced at her calendar. July fifteenth, she thought. Houston's July, their July, was half gone, and they were no closer to establishing a lasting future together than they were when they'd met again on the plane after the two-month separation. It was as though they kept stepping through looking glasses and existing in make-believe worlds. Only their lovemaking was real, earthy, honest.

And that wasn't enough.

What would happen, she wondered, if she told Houston that she loved him? Oh, how she yearned to say the words to the only man she had ever loved. But no, this wasn't the time. Things were too unsettled, off kilter, and she wasn't at all sure of his depth of feeling for her. They'd had so little time together, and so little of it was real!

January rested her elbow on her desk and rested her chin on her hand as she gazed at Houston. So magnificent, she thought wistfully, and she loved him so much. She watched as he closed the file, then reached for another one, flipping it open and beginning to read.

"Holy Toledo," he said, getting slowly to his feet.

The file was in his hands, his eyes riveted on the papers.

"What's wrong?" January said, frowning.

He came around the desk and strode across the room to stand beside her chair. "This is your report on what you did in preparation for decorating January Hall."

"And?"

He blinked, looked at the paper again, then back at her. "You're sending Terry to Paris in the jet to pick up wallpaper that has been specially designed and made at your request? You're paying that fee"—he glanced at the paper again—"to some decorator named Paulo here in Manhattan to take charge of supervising? You sent someone down South to scout for antiques such as knickknacks and pictures, and Terry is to fly in and pick them up? There's a chartered freight barge on standby in Maine waiting to receive all shipments and take them to January Hall?"

"Houston, what is your problem?" she said, getting to her feet. "I took care of every detail with the most expedient methods."

"And the most expensive. Good Lord, look at the cost of all of this."

"So? The funds were available for this project, and I used them. Why take months to do what could be done in days or weeks?"

"You sent a private jet for wallpaper?" he said, an incredulous expression on his face.

"Why not?" she said, throwing up her hands. "It got the job done, didn't it? I want January Hall to be perfect, Houston. I"—she took a deep breath—"I admit I used the advantages available to me as a St.

John to see that everything is going to be as it should be. I'm not flaunting my position, I have a great deal of pride in what I've accomplished, and I know January Hall is going to be a masterpiece. You can say 'Holy Toledo' from here to Sunday, but you won't convince me that I did anything wrong."

Houston stared at her for a long moment, then a slow smile tugged his face. "You're incredible," he said, the smile growing. "You've done it again. You have such an easy, unaffected way of dealing with your wealth that I continually find myself accepting it as the most natural thing to do."

"Then you agree that I did the right thing?"

"I'd be crazy not to. What would have dragged on for months—with possible delays, delivery problems, constant trips back and forth—is going to come together in a week like a fine-tuned machine. Incredible."

"Holy Toledo," January said, smiling at him.

Houston matched her expression, then went back to sit behind his desk, studying the file folder.

"I just wish . . ." January began. "Oh, never mind."

He looked up at her. "You wish what? What's wrong?"

She sighed. "I don't know, Houston. I used to look forward to this time of year when the onslaught of requests for funds came in. It was exhausting, but exhilarating, challenging. This year it's just exhausting. And insulting at times. I just read a fully documented proposal asking for a quarter of a million dollars to train seals to bark—or whatever they do—in code so that secret agents can pass messages to each other. Can you believe that? No one would notice, of course, that the CIA had suddenly developed a penchant for going to the zoo."

Houston chuckled, then laced his hands behind this head and leaned back in his chair. His smile faded slowly, and he moved forward again, crossing his arms on the top of the desk.

"You know," he said thoughtfully, "when I first started working in construction during the summers when I was in high school, I was on a demolition crew. Every summer I saw old buildings torn to the ground, the debris carted away, and an empty lot left, as though nothing had ever been there, no lives ever touched by what had disappeared."

"But something new went up in its place, right?" January said.

"Yeah. I always made it a point to go by the different sites, see what was being built. But I wasn't a part of that. I could only watch. I knew by then that I wanted to work with my hands, be outside, but that it would be on the building end of things, not the tearing down. I like remodelling, too, because it means something is going to be salvaged, improved, given another chance."

"I understand," January said, nodding.

"The point I'm making, January, is that maybe you need a change for a while. I realize that what you're doing is important, that the money you designate goes to projects that could eventually benefit a great many people. But the key word here is *eventually*. How often do you see concrete proof of accomplishment?"

"Very, very rarely. Research projects go on for years. Oh, I receive reports of progress, but . . . no, I can't stand back and say, 'See? I helped do that.' When you help build a house, then later drive by and there are children playing in the yard, flowers by the door, you must have a tremendous sense of pride."

"I do," Houston said, "even after all these years of being in construction. I make very sure I don't lose touch with that part of myself." He paused. "January, don't you think it's time to give yourself that kind of"—he frowned, as though searching for the word he wanted—"gift?"

"What a lovely way to put it," she said.

"Are there other people here capable of doing your job? From what I've seen during this flu fiasco, there's a lot of cross-training at St. John Enterprises."

"My father firmly believed in cross-training, and my mother has always followed that policy. There are two people who could do my job."

"Well, then?"

January got to her feet and walked to the floor-to-ceiling windows. She looked out over the bustling city far below, then turned to face Houston.

"What are you suggesting I do?" she asked.

Houston stood and moved to stand in front of her. "January Hall."

"But . . ."

"That's what you wish, isn't it? To be there, see January Hall transformed into what it will become?"

"Oh, yes, I do. I can see it so clearly in my mind, but I had to get back to my own work. Houston, January Hall is your project."

"Not really. I'm just a temporary employee, remember? I'm filling in for a while like your mother asked me to because of there being so many people out sick. January Hall has reached the point where decorating decisions have to be made. What goes where, that sort of thing."

"But those choices have to be followed up on, and someone besides Paulo has to supervise the other work. Granted, the furniture is just brought in, but the walls, floors, the grounds . . . someone has to be in charge."

Houston ran a restless hand through his hair. "Any good construction man could handle it."

"Houston?" January whispered, searching his face for a clue as to what he was leading up to. "What are you saying?" Was he about to tell her that he was leaving, going home to Chicago? No! Oh, please, no. "Houston?"

He moved around her to stand in front of the windows, shoving his hands into the pockets of his jeans, his back to her. January turned to look at him, seeing the rigid set to his massive shoulders.

"Houston?" she said again, her heart racing.

"I stepped in because you were shorthanded here," he said quietly, still staring out the window, "but most of the people are back now. Plus, what needs to be done at January Hall is standard work. I won't stay on, collecting what are enormous paychecks, because of my relationship with you. I won't take advantage of the fact that I'm your lover, January."

"It wouldn't be like that, Houston," she said, a frantic edge to her voice.

He turned to face her. "Wouldn't it?"

"No."

"Dammit, January," he said, his voice rising, "you could pick up the phone and call a dozen men who could supervise the work at January Hall."

"Is that what you want me to do?" she said, her

voice also rising. "First you suggest that I take a break from my regular routine and concentrate on January Hall. Now you're saying I should find some-one else to go to the island with. Why are you beat-ing around the bush? If you want to go back to Chicago, just say so. Is this it, Houston? Have you finally solved your problem? Have you gotten pesty January St. John out of your system?"

Houston's hands shot up, and he gripped her up-per arms. "No," he said, a pulse beating wildly in his temple. "No, you're not out of my system, not by a long shot." Out? Hell. She was in his heart, his mind, his very soul. Forever. "But, dammit, there hasn't been anything normal about our time to-gether. We just jump from one fantasy world to the next. We're spinning our wheels. I can't continue with this farce, go to the island under the false pretense that I'm the only one qualified to supervise the work at January Hall."

"You're the one St. John Enterprises has hired. What's wrong with that? Do you want to turn that job over to someone else? I thought you cared about January Hall."

"I do!"

"And I thought," January said, her voice trembling, "that you cared about me."

"Ah, damn," Houston said gruffly, then brought his mouth down hard onto hers.

The bruising onslaught of Houston's lips gentled in the next instant as he gathered January close to his body and delved his tongue deep into her mouth. She leaned into him, returning the kiss with total abandon. Their breathing was labored when he fi-nally lifted his head.

"January," he said, his voice gritty, "do you understand what I'm saying? We're working, living, making love together, but it's not quite real. I don't think for one minute that you normally grab a sandwich from a deli for dinner. There's a world out there, a social scene you're accustomed to moving in. None of that is happening."

"We've been busy."

"I know, but that doesn't erase the fact that it's not the lifestyle you're used to. My idea of a great time is going to a baseball game and eating hot dogs on soggy buns. You go to the theater, right? Live theater, and the ballet, eat at four-star restaurants. Right?"

"Yes, but . . is that what you want me to do? Set up evenings like that, drag you along so that you can hate every minute of it? Then you can say, 'See? I told you. We're just too different.' You'd give up on us over theater versus soggy hot dog buns? Do you want me out of your life so badly, you'd use a flimsy excuse like that?"

"You're twisting everything around," Houston said, none too quietly. "You're making me sound like an idiot."

"I'm simply trying to understand what it is that you want. Yes, I realize that things haven't been quite normal, that you don't have a clear picture of how I usually conduct my life. But, dammit, Houston Tyler." Tears misted her eyes. "Do you think going to the theater is more important to me than sharing soggy buns with you?" A sob caught in her throat. "Yes, you are an idiot," she went on, tears spilling onto her cheeks, "because you're too dumb to see that I love you with every breath in my body.

And I hate you because all you're interested in is getting me out of your mind, and that is a rotten thing to do." She swept the tears from her cheeks. "Oh-h-h, dammit! Go take a flying leap." She spun around and started away.

Houston blinked once, then closed the distance between them in two long strides. He grabbed January's arm to stop her flight, then stepped in front of her.

"What did you say?" he said, a wide smile on his face.

"I said, *dammit!*" she yelled. "A very unladylike *dammit*, followed by your taking a long walk off a short pier. Get out of my way, Houston Tyler, or I'll . . . I'll break your nose." Two more tears slid down her cheeks.

"Ah, January," he said, cradling her face in his hands. He wiped away her tears with his thumbs, his smile changing to a gentle, loving expression. "Did you mean it? What you said?"

"No," she said, then sniffled. "I wouldn't break your nose again."

"Do you love me?" he said, his voice low and husky with emotion. "Because, January? I love you, too. I truly do."

"You love me?" she whispered, her eyes wide. "Me? January St. John? In July?"

"You"—he lowered his lips to hers—"are my January in July, and I love you."

Houston brushed his lips over January's, then took full possession of her mouth, his heart racing as well as his mind. January loved him! his brain thundered. Ah, man, he couldn't believe it. *She* loved

JANUARY IN JULY • 113

him, and *he* loved *her*, and everything was *bee-yoo-tee-ful*. What a July! They'd be married . . .

A rush of desire swept through Houston as January met his tongue, causing all rational thought to disappear into a hazy mist of passion. He gathered her close to him, crushing her breasts to his chest as his manhood surged against the zipper of his jeans. He drank in the taste of her, the aroma, the feel of her soft curves nestled to his hard body.

The kiss intensified.

Oh, Houston, January's mind sang, echoed by a joyous song from her heart. He loved her! He wasn't going to dust her out of his mind after all. Her hopes, dreams, everything, were coming true. Houston Tyler loved her! They'd be married . . .

"I want you," Houston murmured, close to her lips. "Lord, how I want you."

"Yes. Oh, goodness, goodness, yes."

"No," he said, raising his head.

"What?" she said, slowly lifting her lashes.

"We're in your office, remember?" He drew a ragged breath, then set her gently away from him.

"Oh." She glanced around. "So we are. Yes, we're standing smack-dab in the middle of my office. Well . . . dammit."

Houston chuckled. "I'm going to have to do something about cleaning up your mouth." He became serious again. "January, I do love you very much. I wanted to tell you, but I wasn't sure when the time was right. Well, now we know . . . we love each other. I want you to be my wife, the mother of my baby."

"Oh, Houston," she said, her eyes filling with tears again. "That's what I want too."

He ran his hand over the back of his neck and frowned. "Yeah, well, we have a lot to figure out, problems to solve."

"We will, Houston, together. What we're facing isn't all that complicated."

"Oh, no? Try totally different lifestyles, incomes, general standards of living. Those are biggies, my magnolia." He shook his head. "Very big biggies."

She ran her hands up his chest to circle his neck. "We don't have to discuss them now, do we? We should celebrate, do something special. In case you didn't notice, Mr. Tyler, we just agreed to become husband and wife. Oh, good gracious, we're getting married!"

Houston smiled, then turned his head as a knock sounded at the door. He tugged at January's arms. She tightened her hold.

"January, there's someone at the door," he said. "Unglue yourself from my body."

"No."

"Lord," he said, pulling her hands from his neck. "Behave yourself." He turned to the door again. "Come in."

Sara St. John entered and smiled at the pair. "Hello, hello," she said, glancing first at January, then Houston. "You two look like I caught you with your hands in the cookie jar. Did I interrupt something?"

"No," Houston said.

"Yes," January said at the same time. Houston glared at her.

Sara laughed. "I definitely interrupted something."

"Mrs. St. John . . ." Houston began, then cleared his throat. "I . . . that is, January and I . . . well, we have a lot to work out, but we . . . what I mean is . . ."

"Oh, for Pete's sake," January said. "Mother, Houston and I are getting married."

"Oh, geez," Houston said, rolling his eyes heavenward. "I was going to break it to her gently."

"Married?" Sara said. "You're in love and you're getting married? Oh, that's splendid."

"I know," January said, beaming.

"It is?" Houston said. "It's splendid?"

"I'm so happy for you both," Sara said. She hugged January, then Houston.

"You are?" Houston said.

"So am I," January said.

"You did it, January," Sara said. "You were a true January, just like we talked about. You've chosen well, my darling."

"She has not!" Houston yelled. Sara and January jumped in surprise. "Isn't anyone paying attention here? We have massive problems. I'm a blue-collar construction worker, remember? I'm middle-class. I'm soggy buns, for crying out loud!"

January burst into laughter. "Oh, good grief."

"Houston," Sara said, merriment dancing in her eyes, "if January is satisfied with the condition of your buns, it's certainly no business of mine."

"Oh, God," Houston said, dropping his face into his hands. He took a deep breath, then looked at Sara again. "Forget the buns," he said through clenched teeth. "Mrs. St. John, I can't support your daughter in the manner to which she is accustomed. We have totally different backgrounds, lifestyles. We come from opposite worlds."

"Oh, so what," Sara said, waving her hand breezily in the air. "I'm not hearing anything that can't be solved. Well, I have a meeting, and I must dash. My blessings, children. I'm thrilled. I'll talk to you later." She hurried from the room.

Houston looked at January. "I don't believe her attitude."

"I do," January said. "Houston, my mother was a waitress in a small café when she met my father, who was already a millionaire. They raised me to judge people as people, not by their financial worth. I knew she wouldn't flicker over the fact that you're a construction worker. She won't give it another thought."

"And you?"

"Houston, I love you. We'll work all this out, you'll see. My parents did it, so why can't we?"

"It's not that simple, January. I've told myself there has to be a way to solve this, but we haven't even had a chance to try. Everything we've done together has been temporary, not the norm."

"I know, but you've seen a few things that go along with my being a St. John; the limousine, the plane, my apartment. You didn't seem to hate them."

"I don't. I really don't."

"See? You can take those off your worry list already," she said, then circled his neck with her arms again. "Oh, I'm so happy. Let's not discuss any more problems, okay? Not today. This is too special, too wonderful. We'll celebrate, go out to dinner, then home to bed. Just the two of us. Just the future Mr. and Mrs. Houston Tyler."

"We have a lot of work stacked up." He sucked in his breath as she wiggled against him. "What about . . . oh, man . . . January Hall?"

"We could do January Hall together, Houston," she said, her lips close to his. "Wouldn't that be fun?"

"Fun," he repeated. "You're driving me out of my mind, lady. Let's get out of here."

"I'm delighted that you suggested that, sir." She gave him a quick peck on the lips. "Let's go home."

At January's apartment, they quickly shed their clothes and tumbled onto the bed, reaching for each other. Their lovemaking held special meaning, spoke of commitment to a lifetime together, forsaking all others. They declared their love over and over as they soared above reality to a place of magical fireworks. Then, in sated contentment, they lay close together in the big bed. Houston slipped his arm under his head and stared up at the ceiling, his other arm holding January close to his side. She fiddled with the moist curls on his chest.

"Where would you like to go to dinner?" January asked finally.

"I don't know. You're the expert, you pick a place. Just remember that I have a very limited wardrobe with me." He paused. "I don't even own a tuxedo, January. If I need one, I rent it for the evening."

She shrugged. "Whatever."

"And I don't have a car, only a pickup truck. And . . . ah, the list is endless. An endless list of what I don't have. So what happens? I ride in your limo, your plane, live in your swanky apartment, and decide that I like it, all of it. What does that make me?"

"Human. There's nothing wrong with enjoying a

limo or a private jet. Goodness, who wouldn't? And they're not really mine. They belong to the company I work for. The company you're working for at the moment."

"You're oversimplifying things."

"No, I'm not. I'm just refusing to allow anything to spoil today. We'll work everything out, Houston, but can't we put it on hold for a few hours?"

"Yeah, okay. I'm sorry."

"Except January Hall. Could we talk about that?"

"I suppose."

"I think you're right about my needing a break from what I usually do. Oh, I'd love to be involved in making January Hall into something wonderful. We could do it together, Houston."

"Go back to the island, be the master and mistress of January Hall as we turn it into a resort?"

"Yes."

"That's fantasy again, January. That's you dressed in jeans and eating makeshift meals. That island is a world apart from the way you usually live. When are we going to face up to the very real difference between us that could cause serious problems?"

She laughed. "The soggy-buns dilemma?"

He chuckled. "You refuse to get serious today, don't you?"

She trailed her fingers down his chest to his stomach, then lower. "Oh, I could get serious about the proper subject."

"Listen, Miss Busy Fingers, you're asking for trouble."

"No, Houston," she whispered. "I'm asking for you. I want you, and oh, mercy, you want me. Come to me. Love me. That's all I'm going to think about."

He pulled her on top of him and sank his hands into her silky curls. "I love you, January St. John. This is a day to remember. A July to remember."

"A lifetime to remember," she said, then met his lips in a searing kiss.

The restaurant that January selected was small, rather plain, but cozy. She wore a yellow gauze dress and sandals and told Houston he needn't bother with a tie. The food was delicious, and January chattered endlessly, jumping from one topic to the next.

Houston only half listened, managing to comment in the appropriate places. He glanced around often, seeing what he realized were average working people treating themselves to dinner out.

Not good, he decided. This place wasn't remotely close to what January would normally choose to celebrate a major event in her life. She had scaled down to Houston's wardrobe and wallet to be sure he wouldn't be embarrassed. She seemed to be having a great time, but like so many other things they'd done together, it wasn't quite real. They were doing the middle-class routine again.

When, he wondered, would January start yearning for the first-class places she'd known all of her life? She was basking in the knowledge that she and Houston truly loved each other and would probably have settled for hot dogs on soggy buns for dinner. But for how long? They had to stop running, had to face facts, weigh and measure, see where they really stood.

January wanted to work with him on January

Hall, he knew, and he wanted that too. Was that wrong? A little more time in a fantasy world? A little more postponing of cold, hard facts? Yeah, it was probably very wrong, but he was going to do it. January Hall had become strangely important to him.

"January," he said, "I think it would be great if we worked together on January Hall."

"Oh, Houston, that's wonderful," she said, her eyes sparkling. "We could . . . well . . ."

"We could what?"

"Spend our honeymoon there."

"What?" he said, his eyes widening.

She frowned. "I guess that was a bit pushy. Well, no, not really. I'm the bride half of the bride and groom. I have the right to an opinion. Okay, here's my opinion. We should get married as soon as possible and spend our honeymoon creating a masterpiece of January Hall."

"That's not a honeymoon, that's work."

"Not if we're doing it together. We can always take a trip later to Hawaii or whatever. Oh, wait. I'm forgetting about your family. They'd probably be crushed if they weren't at your wedding."

"They'd understand. But, January, this is nuts. Don't you want a big, fancy, social wedding like Lady Di?"

"No."

"I don't know," he said, shaking his head. And he *didn't* know. Didn't know if she was telling the truth or, like that restaurant they were in, was paring down to his level of society and economy. It seemed to be getting more tangled and confused by the minute. The only thing that was crystal clear was that he loved January and she loved him. If only, *only*, that were enough. But it wasn't, he knew it, and the knot in his gut was there to remind him if he started to forget. What in the hell was he going to do?

"Houston?"

"What? Oh, I was thinking about what you said."

"And?"

"Let's compromise, okay? We'll work on January Hall together, but we won't get married before we go to the island. It might suit your fancy, but it's not my idea of a honeymoon. With a good crew, it won't take long to get January Hall into shape. We'll need a few days to get organized, get everything lined up to be shipped over there, then we'll go. When January Hall is finished, we'll concentrate on our own plans. Okay?"

"Well, yes, if that's what you want to do. Yes, we'll compromise." She paused. "Oh, I have the perfect idea. We'll be married on our birthdays. On July thirty-first. How's that?"

"Perfect," he said, smiling at her warmly. "You'll be the nicest birthday present I've ever had."

"And you'll be mine. Oh, Houston, I'm so happy, I feel as though I'm going to pop a seam."

"Maybe you just ate too much," he said, laughing. "You sure shoveled it in, kid."

"The food is scrumptious. My parents and I used to come here for homemade pie when I was a little girl."

Houston leaned toward her. "The St. Johns, *the* St. Johns of Manhattan, brought their daughter to this place for pie?"

"Yep. It was one of our favorite outings. I'll be right back. I'm going to the powder room."

As January walked away, Houston glanced around the less-than-fancy restaurant, trying to picture Sara St. John and a faceless man in a five-hundred-dollar suit enjoying pie with their dark-haired little girl.

Was it possible, Houston wondered, that he'd misjudged January in regard to her choice of restaurant to celebrate their special day? Had she picked it, not to meet Houston's pocketbook but because it held sweet memories for her? Had it given her a feeling of sharing her happiness with her deceased father?

Seven

January stood under a tree close to Houston's side with his arm circling her shoulders as the parade of men continued to trek into January Hall with furniture and boxes of various supplies. The late-afternoon sun cast a halo of golden light over the huge, freshly painted structure, transforming it into a creation of beauty.

"It's spectacular," January said.

"*You're* spectacular," Houston said, kissing her on the temple. "I still don't see how you did it. All I had to do was hire crews, a lot of which I found locally. But you? Lord, you had to coordinate decorating ideas for the whole place. The real miracle is that according to the invoices, everything is here."

"It wasn't that difficult, Houston. I'd daydreamed about January Hall so much, it was clear as a picture in my mind. And I'll be the first to admit that I threw the St. John name around a bit to get what I wanted. I hope that prince, or whatever he is, isn't too upset when he finds out the bed he ordered has been sold. Oh, well."

Houston chuckled.

"Uh-oh," January said. "Here comes Paulo. Houston, be nice. You absolutely terrify my cute little decorator. He looks at you like you eat raw meat for breakfast."

Houston hooted with laughter. "I haven't said more than 'Hi, what's doin'?' to the guy."

"He said you growled at him. Shh, be quiet. He's very sensitive."

A small, gray-goateed man in his fifties with a black beret on his head hurried toward them. He wore dark slacks, a satin magenta shirt, and a green scarf puffed at his throat. He eyed Houston warily, then moved to stand by January.

"It's going to be divine," Paulo said, "absolutely divine. I have everything in the ballroom marked for the appropriate rooms. Once the"—he peered around January to glance at Houston—"burly types paper and paint, we can move the furniture right into the rooms. The hardwood floors are divine. The gray carpeting is a decorator's dream. And your choices of furnishings?" He kissed the tips of his fingers. "Absolutely . . ."

"Divine," Houston said pleasantly. January jabbed him in the ribs with her elbow.

"Where did you find him?" Paulo whispered to January. "I can't bear the thought of leaving you alone on this island tonight with that . . . that mountain."

"I'll be fine, darling," January said, patting Paulo's hand. "Houston and I are going to be married, remember?"

"Please, don't remind me. You're marrying a tree, a redwood tree."

"A what?" Houston said.

"Paulo, did you do as I asked?" January said.

The decorator sighed dramatically. "Yes, I did. Against my better judgment, of course, but it's everything you requested. And because it has my touch, it's perfection personified."

"Oh, brother," Houston muttered.

"Last boat is leaving," someone yelled.

"Merciful saints, I must be on it," Paulo said. "It's bad enough I have to spend the night in some inn that never heard of French onion soup, but it's better than being stuck out here. I'll see you tomorrow." He kissed the air near January's cheek. "Ta-ta, darling." He scurried away.

"Very, very weird," Houston said.

"He's cute," January said. "He tells everyone he's French, but he's actually Polish and from New Jersey. Cute as a button and very talented." She watched as the last of the men disappeared from view, then turned to Houston. "Alone at last," she said, smiling up at him.

He pulled her close. "Now I'll have my wicked way with you, my magnolia."

"I certainly hope so, suh."

He kissed her hard and long, and January's knees were trembling when he finally released her. Houston drew a steadying breath, then glanced around.

"It's so peaceful here," he said quietly. "This place has really cast a spell over me. I have a feeling that I'm going to be hovering around that crew like a mother hen, making sure everything is perfect. You'd think I was supervising work on my own home, instead of what will be a resort for strangers. But it's just . . . really something."

January looked up at Houston as he continued to gaze at January Hall. She glanced at the house, then back at Houston's face, seeing the admiration in his eyes as he surveyed the majestic structure.

"You really are sentimental," she said, smiling at him warmly.

"Naw, I'm a tree. A big, old, thick redwood tree. A hungry tree, in fact. Let's go inside and see what's in that picnic basket they fixed us at the inn."

"You're on. We even have a kitchen table and chairs to use. All the comforts of home."

"Home," Houston said as they started forward. "That's the feeling I get when I come here. Lord, that's nuts."

January didn't comment as she entered the house with Houston. The ballroom, off to the left, was crammed with furniture and boxes, and she registered a tremendous sense of anticipation at the thought of the transformation that would come over January Hall in the next few days.

It would be a beautiful home, she mused. No, no, now Houston had *her* doing it. It wasn't going to be a home, it was a resort, a hotel. But at that moment it was hard to imagine strangers sitting on the furniture she had chosen with such loving care, sleeping in the bedrooms, each of which would be unique and typical of the Southern plantation days.

"Food," Houston said as they entered the kitchen. "Ah, there's the basket."

January laughed. "I'll get us something to drink. Sit. I'd hate to have you pass out from hunger."

They were soon enjoying crispy fried chicken, potato salad, flaky biscuits, and home-canned peaches, along with a strong ale that Houston was convinced had been brewed in someone's basement.

"Delicious," he said, reaching for another piece of chicken. "I assume when you asked cute, divine Paulo if he'd done as you asked, you were referring to his having a bed set up for us?"

"Yes," January said, nodding.

"As thick as the carpeting is, we could have slept in sleeping bags on the floor, but a bed will be put to good use."

"Oh?"

"Sleep, you know? I'm very tired, very tired. This has been a long, hard day, my magnolia. It's not easy being the master of a plantation. Rough work, but someone has to do it." He yawned dramatically. "But, lawd, it does take a lot out of a man. I do believe I'll be headin' for that bed mighty early."

"Do tell," January said, then laughed.

He leaned toward her, grinning. "I'm *trying* to tell you, Magnolia. I'm hot for your body."

January gasped, covering her heart with her hand, and batted her eyelashes. "My stars, suh, you are upsetting my sensibilities. Y'all can't say such things to a Southern lady. I'll have an attack of the vapors. One does not speak of the urges and needs of one's . . . um . . . self."

They dissolved in laughter, and the happy sound bounced off the walls and seemed to fill the room to overflowing. They decided to save the last of the biscuits and peaches for breakfast, then wandered through the house as darkness fell. Outside the master suite, January stopped.

"Houston," she said, looking up at him, "would you give me a half an hour?"

He shrugged. "No problem. I'll go back downstairs and line up some of the wallpaper in the order it's to be used."

She gave him a quick kiss. "Thank you," she said, then entered the bedroom and closed the door behind her.

In exactly thirty minutes, Houston was standing outside the bedroom door, staring at the closed wooden panel.

Should he knock? he wondered. Knock, hell, that was *their* room, his and January's. And she was *his* lady. He sure as hell didn't have to ask permission to enter. He'd be damned if he'd knock.

Rolling his eyes heavenward in self-disgust, he knocked on the door.

"Come in."

"Gosh and golly, thanks a heap," he mumbled sarcastically. He opened the door, stepped inside, and stopped, absently closing the door behind him. "Oh . . . Lord," he said, his heart thundering.

The large room was glowing from the light of a dozen candles set on the dresser and nightstands. The king-size bed was turned back, revealing pale blue sheets and fluffy pillows.

And standing by the bed was January.

She was dressed in a filmy white nightgown that flowed around her like a transparent cloud. The candlelight flickered over her, giving glimpses of her naked body beneath the sheer material. She had a soft, loving smile on her face.

Houston could hardly breathe. The blood pounded in his veins, and heat gathered low in his body as he drank in the sight of the vision of loveliness standing before him. He felt a strange tightening in his throat, as though he were about to cry as he filled his senses with all that was January St. John, the woman he loved.

"You," he said, his voice raspy, "are the most beautiful woman on the face of this earth. "I . . . I love you."

"Oh, Houston, I love you, too," she said, her voice trembling. "I wanted to surprise you with this room—Paulo helped me—and . . . oh, please come over here before I faint dead away."

Houston walked slowly toward her, very slowly, his heated gaze visually tracing every inch of her as he closed the distance between them.

The sexuality, the awareness, the man seeing the essence of his woman, the woman seeing her man, all virtually crackled in the air. The sense of anticipation built, hummed, caused hearts to race and desire to pulse deep within bodies consumed by waves of passion.

Houston stopped in front of January, and their eyes met, smoky with need, sending and receiving messages of desire.

The candlelight poured over them with a warming embrace, seeming to lift them from the here and now and transport them back in time. The master of January Hall raised his hands to gently cradle the face of the mistress of the land where they shared their lives and their love. He swept her into his arms and placed her on the bed, standing tall and massive above her as his gaze once more traveled over her, igniting her passion further as he etched her indelibly in his mind. With shaking hands he shed his clothes, then skimmed the filmy gown from January's body.

Houston stretched out next to her but didn't touch her as he strove for control.

"Thank you for this," he said, his eyes darting around the room. "I'll never forget this night."

"Nor will I. Love me, Houston. I want you so much."

It was a merging of senses, of bodies, a joining of souls. It was all, and it was more, than they had ever shared before. It was giving and receiving. It held a mysterious aura of a long-ago time, and every promise of the future to come.

It was January and Houston.

It was ecstasy.

The candles burned low. The shadows darkened over the lovers who rode the tides of passion to heights beyond description in their magnitude and beauty. Time and again they reached for each other; wanting, needing, giving, taking. Loving.

Then as the last candle flickered and died, the master and mistress of January Hall slept.

"Divine, divine, divine," Paulo cooed, as he came into the kitchen. "I must say, January, for a muscle-bound mountain, your Houston does seem to have a rather high level of intelligence. He handles his crew like an expert."

"He *is* an expert," January said. "At a lot of things."

"Don't be tacky, darling. I detest details of people's

love lives. Anyway, the work is progressing beautifully. This house is divine. No, that's not a good enough word. It's magnificent. I may vacation at January Hall myself in the future."

January looked up quickly from where she sat at the table checking invoices. "You'd come here as a guest?"

"Yes, I believe I would. Everything is of the highest quality, I adore the Southern plantation effect, and I assume you'd hired a respectable chef. Do be sure he can make French onion soup. Why are you frowning?"

"I'm just being silly, Paulo. I've become so attached to January Hall, it's hard to see it as a resort, a hotel. I picture it as a home, mine and Houston's."

Paulo shrugged. "So keep it as your home. There's no law that says you have to turn it into a hotel. Cancel your advertising plans, and that's that. Lord knows you can afford the place. Actually I like that idea. You can invite me for a weekend as your guest, and it won't cost me a cent. I'll mooch."

January laughed. "Shame on you. I'd expect you to bring a very expensive bottle of wine."

"You've got a deal. Are you really serious about this, January? Would you consider canceling the plans to make January Hall a hotel?"

She sighed. "No, I guess not. I'm just daydreaming. It's become so special to me, and Houston says he feels as though he's home when he comes here." She plunked her elbow on the table and rested her chin in her hand. "I could work here, of course. I'd bring the files for requests for grants and endowments and . . . but Houston would be bored out of his mind."

"Not necessarily," Paulo said. "There's a lot of new development going on in this part of Maine. Not only that, there are old homes constantly in need of repair. I'd say your mountain could be a very busy boy."

"Really?" January said, straightening. She plopped her chin back in her hand. "Quit talking to me, Paulo. You're getting me all charged up over something that is ridiculous." She paused. "Isn't it?"

"Is it?" he said, winking at her. "I must go check on my charges. Things fall apart when the genius isn't on the scene. Ta-ta, love."

January watched him leave the kitchen, a frown now on her face. "Darn you, Paulo," she said aloud. She'd been getting herself in enough mental trouble with her daydreaming without someone aiding and abetting her fantasies. She and Houston could not, she told herself, live at January Hall. They simply couldn't chuck the plans to turn it into a hotel and make it their home. Or could they?

Why not? she pondered. All she had to do was purchase January Hall and the island from St. John Enterprises with her own money and—bingo!—it would belong to Mr. and Mrs. Houston Tyler. No, Houston probably wouldn't allow that. His pride could very well stand in the way of her buying their home for them.

Unless . . .

January stiffened in her chair again, her mind racing as an idea grew from a niggling thought to a full-blown plan.

"Yes? No?" she said, pressing her hands to her cheeks. "Oh, I just don't know."

"Don't know what, Magnolia?" Houston said as he entered the kitchen.

"Well, suh, I'm just not at all sure if I love y'all. I mean, do I or don't I? Do you have an opinion on the matter, suh?"

Houston chuckled, then scooped January out of her chair and held her tightly in his arms.

"You love me," he said, close to her lips.

"Why, suh, I do believe you are right. Perhaps you should kiss me just so I'm certain of that fact."

"My pleasure, ma'am."

The kiss was long and powerful, and January's cheeks were flushed when Houston finally lifted his head and set her on the edge of the table. He planted his hands on either side of her hips, trapping her in place as he leaned close to her.

"Did that answer your question?" he said.

"I must say, it did," she said, then drew a wobbly breath. "Goodness. Yes, master of January Hall, I love y'all to pieces, I swear I do."

Houston straightened, a grin on his face. "You're a cuckoo, but I love you too."

"How's the work going? Paulo is terribly impressed with you."

"He is? Paulo is impressed with me? Good Lord, January, I can't tell you what that does for my peace of mind. I mean, land's sake, the twit is impressed."

"Stop it," she said, laughing. She whopped him on the arm. "Paulo is . . ."

"Cute. Divine. Yeah, I know. Actually he's okay, once you get used to him. He doesn't waste any time, I'll give him that. He's setting up rooms right behind us. January Hall is coming together like a picture book."

"I've been peeking around corners, keeping out of everyone's way. Oh, Houston, everything is so beautiful."

"Yeah, it really is. The living room is finished, even down to the knickknacks on the tables. I like that room with the grouping in front of the stone fireplace. I was glad to see that you picked some good-sized pieces of furniture."

"Oh?" January said, looking at him intently.

"Yeah, well, what I mean is, I'm not the only big man in the world. There's bound to be some guys staying here when it's a hotel that wouldn't fit in those funny little puffy chairs."

"I was thinking of you when I chose those larger pieces. The truth is, Houston, I was thinking of you, us, when I made *all* the selections. I can't help it. In my mind, my heart, January Hall is ours. You said it yourself. It's as though we've come home."

Houston walked to the window and braced his large hands on the frame, looking out over the land.

"I know," he said quietly, "but it's time to stop daydreaming. We'll be finished here in a couple of days, and then we'll leave. The landscaping crew is coming in after we're gone." He turned to face her. "We're going back to New York very soon, January. We're going to face the facts we've been running from and figure out how in the hell we're going to fit our lives together. Right now I don't have any answers to how we're going to do that. I wish that our loving each other meant that all our problems were automatically solved, but that's another dream."

"Do you hate New York?"

"No, that isn't the issue. I'm sure I could find work there, but that doesn't erase the fact that my

aycheck wouldn't cover the electric bill at your apartment, let alone anything else."

"Oh, Houston, that doesn't matter. I don't care if
ou—"

"Houston!" someone yelled from outside the kitchen
oor. "We need you here."

"Yeah! Coming." He started toward the door, then
oubled back and dropped a quick kiss on Janu-
ry's lips. "I'm going to marry you, January St. John,"
e said fiercely. "I have no intention of letting you
o. I just don't see any answers to our problems
et."

"We'll find them. We will, Houston."

"Yeah," he said, striding toward the door. He
topped again and turned to look at her. "Magnolia?"

"Suh?"

"Do you think that on July thirty-first, on the day
e're married, you could remember to wear your
hoes?"

"Well, mercy me, I'll do my best."

Houston laughed and left the kitchen. A silence
ll, and January swung her legs back and forth as
he remained perched on the edge of the table. Her
aze swept over the huge kitchen, then lingered on
he view beyond the window. With a sigh she slid
er bare feet to the floor, sat down in the chair, and
esumed work on the invoices.

uly 22

January stood in front of January Hall, gazing at
he gleaming structure as the morning sun bathed
t in bright light. She wrapped her hands around
er elbows and hugged herself tightly, as though

protecting the precious memories she'd gathered during her stay on the island with Houston.

Oh, heavens, she thought frantically, she didn't want to leave. She wanted to send the boat that was waiting for them away, then fling herself into Houston's arms and beg him to stay at January Hall with her. She didn't want to go back to New York, to reality, to all the problems they faced.

"January?" Houston called, coming around the side of the house.

"Yes, I'm here."

Houston came to where she stood, and she managed a weak smile.

"Hey," he said, "why so glum? You should be bursting with pride over the way January Hall turned out."

"I am. It's just that I . . . I don't want to leave here."

He drew his thumb over her cheek. "I know. I understand, I really do. There's something magical about this place, isn't there? It's as though it had dropped out of the heavens just for us."

"Houston, is the landscaping crew still coming in tomorrow?"

"Yes. Your expert from St. John Enterprises will be in charge. It will only take them a couple of days to have the grounds shipshape. It's amazing what those guys can do."

"Well, I was thinking . . . wondering . . ." Her voice trailed off.

"What? Come on, talk to me."

"Houston, could we be married here at January Hall?"

Houston frowned slightly in surprise. "Here? You want to fly back to the island for the wedding?"

"Oh, yes. Yes, I do, very much. Listen," she rushed on, "we could send Terry and the plane for your family, if you'd like that. Would you? I don't want anything big and flashy, just our loved ones with us. I'll ask my mother, of course, and my aunt and uncle. But we could bring all of your family and—"

"Whoa!" he said, raising his hand. "In the first place . . . no, we're not sending the plane for my family. I want them to meet you, but it will be when I can take you to Chicago. But as far as getting married here at January Hall? Yes, I'd like that."

"Oh, Houston, thank you."

"See? Compromise. My family gets a phone call, but the wedding will be here. Okay?"

"Yes," she said, smiling up at him.

"Wedding," he repeated, running his hand over the back of his neck. "Lord, sometimes I wonder if I'm out of my mind."

January blinked. "Well, thanks a bunch, Tyler."

He pulled her to him, wrapping his arms around her as she leaned her head on his chest.

"You know I love you, want you to be my wife," he said gruffly. "We're to be married on July thirty-first, in a handful of days. I think about it, and I can hardly wait for the hours to pass. But, January? Nothing is solved. There are moments when I panic, feel as though it's foolish, selfish, to go into a marriage with unsolved problems. It *is* foolish. But where are we going to get the answers in less than ten days?"

"We'll compromise . . . somehow. It works for everything else. We haven't really had a chance to try to figure things out. Houston, there's a party tomorrow night that I'm invited to. Everyone who is anyone will be there. We'll go, okay? Together. You'll see that they're just people."

"Right," he said dryly. "I'll be there in my rented tuxedo."

"So? Will you go?"

"Yeah, I'll go. I have to. It's time to pay the piper, see the social scene you move in. What do you think your fancy friends are going to say when I tell them I'm a construction worker?"

"I don't care what they say."

"Well, dammit, I do. Their first thought will be that I'm after your money. What am I supposed to do? Wear a sign around my neck that says, 'I really love January St. John'? They'll be talking about you behind your back, deciding you got suckered in by a dumb laborer with a set of muscles. You're a St. John. You have a reputation to protect, a name."

"Oh-h-h,' she said, narrowing her eyes, "you are really starting to make me mad. What would happen if we went to a party with your friends? Wouldn't there be some who would snicker, say that the bored little rich girl decided to play around beneath her station for something new and exciting to do?"

"Of course not." He paused. "Or . . . at least I don't think they'd come to that conclusion. But then again . . . hell!"

"See? It works both ways. Then what about your reputation? Your family name? 'Did you hear about Houston Tyler? He's the new plaything of a rich Manhattan socialite. Can you believe it? What a fool. What then, Houston?"

"Stop it," he said, gripping her upper arms.

"Houston, you have to look at the whole picture, realize that people will stand in judgment on both sides of the fence. We have to make up our minds that we don't care what any of them think. It's our lives, our marriage, our future. We have to reach a middle ground for ourselves, no one else."

"How?" he said, giving her a small shake. "Suppose we do manage to ignore what everyone is saying. Fine. Then it's just you and me looking at each other over that fence. Where in the hell is this wonderful middle ground you're talking about?"

"I don't know yet," she yelled. "It's up to us to find it."

"Where?" he said, dropping his hands from her arms. "I could work for a year and still not have enough to pay the rent on your apartment."

"There is no rent. I own it."

"Oh, great," he said, throwing up his hands. "Super. You *own* an apartment overlooking Central Park. Well, guess what, Magnolia? I *own* a four-year-old pickup truck. That's it. Zip. Zilch. Nothing else. It doesn't balance out very well, does it?"

"It doesn't matter!"

"Ah, hell, we're just going in circles. Let's get out of here. The boat is waiting. It's time to go back to reality, January." He moved around her and started away.

January took a shuddering breath and pressed her fingertips to her lips, willing herself not to cry. She stared at January Hall, gathered her strength, lifted her chin, and followed Houston. Before January Hall was lost to her view, she turned for one last lingering look at the majestic home.

•   •   •

July 23

Houston sipped the warm, flat champagne in his glass, decided he didn't want it, and plunked the glass on the tray carried by a passing uniformed waiter.

"Another drink, sir?" the waiter asked.

"No. No thank you."

"Very good, sir."

Very good, sir? Houston repeated in his mind. What a dumb thing to say. If he'd taken another drink, would the waiter have clicked his tongue and said, "Very bad, sir"? No, guess not.

Houston glanced around the enormous room, trying to tune out the high volume of noise. There were well over a hundred people at the party, he surmised, all decked out in their finery. Well, January St. John was the most beautiful woman in the place. She looked sensational in her floor-length satin dress that was the color of the sea. So sensational, in fact that he hadn't dared touch her while they were in her apartment, or they never would have gotten to the party.

The party, Houston mused. Actually it wasn't so bad. The food was great, and everyone January had introduced him to was cordial and friendly. Word had spread quickly that January and Houston were to be married, and the hostess had called for quiet so she could make a toast to the bride and groom. He and January had been at this shindig for about two hours now and . . . yeah, okay, it wasn't so bad. January had been dragged off ten minutes before to see some fancy new coat or something the hostess had gotten in London. But all in all, it was so far . . . so good.

Houston glanced down at his rented tuxedo, decided he looked as good as any man in the room, was glad he'd remembered to get a haircut, then smiled politely at a passing woman, who gave him the once-over.

"Damn that January," the woman muttered. "She gets all the good stuff."

Houston nearly choked as he swallowed a burst of laughter. There were naughty and nice there, he admitted. Just as there were at middle-class gatherings. Except for the home they were in and the cost of their clothes, there wasn't much difference when he viewed them just as people. He'd even had a brief conversation with a couple of guys about the current baseball season. So far . . . so good.

"So, you're January's hunk," a man said, bringing Houston from his reverie.

Houston looked at the man beside him. He was tall, thin, blond, about thirty, good-looking, and drunk. Very drunk.

"Name is Todd Manchester," the man said.

"Houston Tyler."

"That's Manchester, Tyler," Todd said, his speech slurred. "Mean anything to you?"

"Can't say that it does."

"Figures. The name Manchester is right up there with St. John in this town."

"That's nice," Houston said, glancing around the room.

"Look at me when I'm talking to you, Tyler. Or don't they teach construction workers manners? No time for that, I suppose. You're too busy pumping up your muscles."

Uh-oh, Houston thought. This joker had better put a cork in it.

"Let me tell you something," Todd said, weaving on his feet. "January is mine. Everyone knows that. It was understood years ago that Todd Manchester would marry January St. John and merge our holdings."

"January apparently has other ideas on the subject," Houston said. "Why don't you give it a rest? You've had too much to drink."

"Don't patronize me, you scum. You've got no business being with January St. John. What do you plan to do? Laugh all the way to the bank as you take over her money?"

"That's all, Manchester," Houston said, a muscle jumping along his jaw. "Back off. January is headed this way. She doesn't need to hear this garbage."

"I'll just bet you don't want her to hear it," Todd said, poking Houston in the chest with a finger. "She might start thinking about why you're really hanging around."

Houston glanced quickly at January, who had quickened her step and was frowning as she made her way toward the two men.

"Manchester," Houston said tightly, looking at him again, "get your hands off me and close your damn mouth."

"You stay away from January St. John," Todd said. He pushed against Houston's chest with the flat of his hand.

"Oh, hell," Houston said.

He pulled back his arm, made a fist, and delivered

a stunning blow to Todd's flushed face. Todd crumbled into a heap on the floor.

"Houston!" January yelled. She hurried to his side as the crowd gasped.

"I'm sorry, Magnolia," Houston said, "but I'm afraid I just broke a Manchester nose."

Eight

Houston entered January's apartment with such
heavy, thudding steps that a delicate figurine on an
end table teetered precariously before settling back
in place. He flung his tuxedo jacket roughly onto a
chair, raked a hand through his hair, then began to
pace, a deep scowl on his face.

January moved through the large living room, turning on lights, keeping one eye on a fuming Houston,
and trying desperately not to smile. To laugh, she
decided, could very well be hazardous to her health,
and even a smile was risky.

"Don't you laugh," Houston said, stopping to point
a long finger at her. "Don't even smile. Damn it,
January, this isn't funny. I saw in the limo that you
were about to fall apart. I'm warning you, don't
laugh."

"I wouldn't dream of it. Nope, not one teeny smile
will form on my luscious lips." She plucked an imag-

inary thread from her dress to hide the merriment she knew was dancing in her eyes. "One does not laugh at heroes. No, suh, we bow deeply when they cross our paths."

"Knock it off!"

"That, suh, seems to be *your* specialty."

"January . . ." he said, a menacing tone to his voice.

She pursed her lips together and clutched her hands primly in front of her, striving for a pose of pure innocence that failed miserably.

Houston shot her another stormy look and resumed his pacing. "The guy was a twit, a foul-mouthed, blithering, drunk twit. I could have handled it . . . maybe . . . if he'd kept his hands off me. No, I probably would have hit him, anyway. He was saying lousy things about you, me, us. But, oh, Lord"—he threw up his hands—"why did I have to hit him? I busted his damn nose, for God's sake."

"Indeed you did, suh," January said pleasantly, then quickly pursed her lips together again as a bubble of laughter threatened to escape.

"January," he said, stopping in front of her. He towered above her, his hands planted on his hips.

"Suh?" she said sweetly.

"Would you stop that? Don't you realize what happened tonight? I made it very clear to over one hundred people, as well as myself, that I don't fit into your social scene. I've probably made you the laughingstock of Manhattan. January St. John's big, muscle-bound dummy decked Todd Manchester at a party. Wonderful. Just wonderful. The twit will probably sue me too. Well, no big deal. All he'll get is a pickup truck. But, dammit, I blew it! Why you're so close to laughing, I'll never know. Are you hysterical? Laughing instead of crying? Laughing instead of shooting me?"

That did it. January couldn't contain her merriment one moment longer. She burst into laughter and sank onto a chair, holding her stomach as she gasped for breath.

"I'm not understanding you again," Houston roared, "but I'm in no mood *not* to understand you. So zip it! Now!"

"Oh, my," January said, struggling for control. "I'm trying. I really am. There. I'm serious. See my serious little face?" She puffed out her cheeks and crossed her eyes.

"You're definitely hysterical. I've blown the St. John name to smithereens, and you know it."

"Houston, for heaven's sake," she said, smiling at him, "would you calm down? You were so angry and upset that you weren't paying attention to what was going on. You just wanted out of there and nearly trampled three people getting to the door. Do you recall a man coming up to you and shaking your hand?"

"No." He paused. "Yeah, vaguely, now that you mention it."

"That was Todd's father!"

"What?"

"I'm not kidding. He was beaming, said it was time that someone took Todd down a peg or two, and he wanted to shake the hand of the man who had done it."

"What?"

"I also heard things like, 'Way to go, Houston' and 'Glad you're one of us, Tyler.' They probably would have had a group toast for you if you hadn't barreled out of there so fast."

"What?"

"Todd Manchester is a spoiled, self-centered brat. We all have put up with him for years, and for the life of me I can't figure out why. We just never questioned the fact that he'd be at every party and we'd have to grin and bear him. It took you to make everyone realize that we don't have to put up with Todd just because he's a Manchester. Oh, you fit in tonight, Houston Tyler. You taught us all a valuable lesson. Money doesn't give anyone the right to be less than human. You were the hero of the evening, and I'm so proud of you, I could burst."

Houston blinked. "What?"

"Is your record stuck?"

"You're not making sense. It's one thing to deck a loudmouth in a sleazy bar, but at a high-society party? Are you nuts?" He shook his head in disbelief.

January stood and moved close to him, circling his neck with her arms. "That's the point, Houston. We're just people. Some good, some bad. Somewhere along the line we got caught up in our own pecking order, and Todd Manchester was given carte blanche to do as he pleased. You . . . you construction worker, you . . . showed us how wrong we were. I thank you on behalf of everyone there tonight."

"January, I broke the guy's nose!"

"I know," she said, laughing. "He was wailing as though he were dying."

"Well, it's painful. I should know. You clobbered my nose, remember?"

"I'll never forget it. What a team we are. Anyone messes with us, we'll pop 'em in the schnozzola."

Houston grinned. "You're a loony tune."

"And you're wonderful, and I love you, and it's time to go to bed. Houston, before that fiasco with Todd happened, were you having a good time at the party?"

"Yeah, I was fine. Most of the people were really very nice."

"See? Houston, we don't have a problem on a social scale. There were men there tonight who would love to go to a baseball game with you and eat hot dogs on soggy buns. *I'd* go to a baseball game with you. It's compromise time again. We'd go to some outings dressed to the teeth and put on our jeans for others. We've found the middle ground on this one, Houston. We really have."

He nodded slowly. "Maybe you're right."

"I know I am. Now can we go to bed?"

"Are you saying you're hot for my body, Magnolia?"

"You bet your soggy buns I am, Tyler."

Houston laughed and lifted her into his arms. "Shame on you."

They made sweet, sensuous love, then January curled up close to Houston and drifted off to sleep, her hand resting on his chest. Houston fiddled with her curls as he stared up into the darkness, one arm beneath his head.

It had been a helluva night, he decided. Confusing, to say the least. He busts a twit's nose and the guy's father shakes his hand? Weird. But the bottom line was, he'd accepted, and had been accepted by, the majority of the people in January's social set. That problem apparently had been solved.

That left, he realized, only the issue of money, of supporting January in the manner to which she was accustomed. Where was the middle ground about money? He bought the tickets to the baseball game, she footed the bill for the evening at the theater? Not good. Yeah, okay, he liked the limousine and the private plane. He wasn't being a total hard-nose about this. But an apartment across from Central Park where he'd live rent-free? No way. He could see the horror on the doorman's face when Houston strolled in wearing grungy jeans, a T-shirt, and a hard hat.

The apartment was nice, really nice, he admitted. But a man wanted to provide a home for his wife. Right. He'd take January to a little boxy house in the suburbs, then watch the limo pull up every morning to drive her to St. John Enterprises. Dammit, where in the hell was the middle ground on the issue of money?

Houston sighed, ran his hand down his face, then kissed January on the forehead. Lord, how he loved her, he mused. He had only a handful of days left to figure all of this out because, oh, yes, he intended to marry his January in July. On July thirty-first at January Hall, January St. John would become Mrs. Houston Tyler.

But then what? his mind screamed. Ah, man, then what?

July 24

The ringing of the telephone woke both January and Houston early the next morning. Houston fumbled in the semidarkness and snatched up the receiver.

"Yeah?"

"Houston?"

"Yeah."

"It's Dallas."

Houston sat bolt-upright, instantly wide-awake. "Hey, bruddah, what's doin'? I just talked to you a few days ago to tell you I'm getting married. This call is costing you a bundle."

"Houston, Dad broke his leg."

"What?"

"Houston, is something wrong?" January said.

"Mom called me," Dallas went on. "Dad was cleaning the leaves out of the eaves troughs at the house and slipped off the ladder. Mom didn't want to bother you so close to your wedding day. But, Houston, she's coming unglued. She can't handle something like this, you know that. Austin and Sam are still on their honeymoon cruise."

"How bad is Dad?" Houston said.

"Houston?" January said.

"He's in the hospital. They had to put a pin in his leg. He's going to be all right, but he'll be laid up for a while, that's for sure. The whole thing has Mom totally rattled. I don't know what to do. If I ask for time off, I'll lose this job for sure, and I need to stay on it so the medical insurance will kick in. I have to be prepared in case Willie has an asthma attack. Dammit, I feel as though I'm being pulled in two. Mom needs me, but so do my wife and son."

"Listen to me, Dallas," Houston said. "You stay there in Tucson. I'll fly home today and take care of the folks."

"But you're getting married in a few days."

"There's plenty of time. Dad is tough, he'll bounce right back. Mom just needs a steadying hand for a while. She's not terrific in a crisis. I'll calm her down, make her see that everything is going to be fine, and be back in time to be married right on schedule. No sweat."

"Are you sure?"

"Positive. I'll call Mom and tell her I'm on my way. I'll phone you tonight and give you a report."

"I hate dumping this on you, Houston."

"You take care of Joyce and Willie. I'll handle this."

"Thanks, bruddah. Thanks doesn't cut it, but—"

"Enough. I'll call you tonight. 'Bye."

"Houston?" January said as he replaced the receiver.

"My father broke his leg. He'll be all right, but my mother is one of those people who doesn't deal very well with anything unpleasant. She just ignores whatever it is until it's over. She's all alone right now, and she really can't handle this. I have to get there and reassure her that everything is going to be okay. I know my dad, January. He'll come through this like a champ. I'll be back in time for the wedding."

"I understand. I saw your father at the institute, remember? It's hard to imagine him laid up. Do you want me to go with you?"

"No, you stay here and do whatever brides do to get ready for their wedding."

"I'll call Terry and tell him to get the plane ready."

"No, I . . . yeah, okay, it's the best way to do it. You know, I had finally decided to swallow my pride and have Terry go get my family so they could be at our wedding. I really did want them to . . . well, so be it." He flipped back the blankets and got out of the bed, striding naked toward the bathroom. "I'll bring my other clothes back with me. I really do own more than a handful of things." He stopped at the bathroom door and turned to face her. "I'm sorry about this, but I do have to go."

"Oh, Houston, I realize that, and I'm so sorry your family won't be at the wedding. I'll miss you terribly, but I certainly understand why you have to go. I'll call Terry, then phone for the limo. I'll fix you something to eat too."

"I love you, January. I'll be back in time for the wedding, I promise. My dad won't knuckle under to a mere broken leg for long. July thirty-first will be our day."

"I love you, too, Houston," she whispered.

Their eyes met and held for a long moment, then Houston went into the bathroom and shut the door. January reached for the phone, made the necessary calls, then pulled on a satin robe and headed for the kitchen to make Houston's breakfast.

Darn it, she thought as she scrambled eggs, she didn't want Houston to go. Just because she understood that he was needed at home didn't mean she had to like the fact that he was leaving. That was fair enough reasoning. Well, he would be back in time for their wedding. She'd be Houston's January in July.

Married to Houston, she thought as she made toast. Married? But they hadn't solved all of their problems yet, hadn't found the middle ground for everything. Hopefully, after the fiasco at the party, Houston now saw that the social circle she moved in wasn't an obstacle in their path. Oh, what a party.

Oh, how gloriously Houston had broken Todd's nose. Pow! Fantastic.

But she knew there were still unsettled issues. Houston was making remarks more and more frequently about his lack of income compared to hers, about the material things she possessed lined up against what he owned. She didn't know what to say when he went off on a tangent about that except her now standard "It doesn't matter!" which got her nothing more than a dark glare from Houston.

"Oh, dear," January said with a sigh. Each minute, hour, day between now and their wedding was precious time needed to solve the remaining problem, find the middle ground for the fact that she was a St. John and Houston was a construction worker. She knew and understood that Houston had to go to Chicago, but his leaving was causing a rush of panic to wash over her. They couldn't solve things together if they weren't together, and they wouldn't be together because Houston wouldn't be there to be together with. "Huh?" she said aloud. "I think I'm confusing myself."

January glanced up as Houston strode into the kitchen dressed in slacks and a knit shirt, his thick auburn hair damp from his shower. Her pulse skittered as she gazed at him, and all thoughts of unsolved problems fled from her mind.

"Terry is getting the plane ready," she said. "The car will be waiting downstairs, and your breakfast is fixed."

"Thank you. And thank you for being so understanding about this. My mother is a sweetheart, but she operates from a different place than the rest of us. Austin says our mother knows how to smile at life."

"That's a lovely way to put it," January said, setting the food on the table.

Houston chuckled. "Well, when you realize that our mother named us Houston, Dallas, and Austin because she's a devoted fan of John Wayne's, and she sees him as the Texan of all Texans, you can sort of get the picture of where she's coming from. There isn't one among us, especially my father, who would have her be any other way than she is. I'm just sorry the timing is so lousy."

"Don't worry about it, Houston. I'll make all the arrangements for the wedding. There are only going to be a few of us at January Hall for the ceremony. I'll take care of the details. You just be sure and show up on time to say 'I do.' "

"I'll be there, Magnolia. But, January, we haven't solved—"

"And there isn't time right now," she interrupted. "Eat. Your parents need you, Houston. That is top-priority at the moment."

A short time later Houston stood by the door and pulled January into his arms. He kissed her until she was trembling in his embrace, then, with the promise to call her that night, he left the apartment.

January stood statue-still as desire hummed throughout her. She missed him already, she realized, and he'd been gone about four or five seconds. Oh, heavens, how long and lonely the days and nights ahead were going to be without Houston Tyler by her side.

• • •

July 27

Sara St. John frowned at her daughter. "You're sure you want to do this, January?"

"Yes, Mother, I am. It's the answer, I'm positive. Houston was called home, and we lost precious time that we needed. So . . . yes, this is good, it really is."

Sara sighed. "I wish I felt that confident about it, but it's really not my place to express an opinion. You know I wish only for you and Houston to be happy together."

"We *are* going to be happy."

"Yes, of course you are. How is Houston's father doing?"

"He's progressing nicely. Houston says his mother will calm down once Mr. Tyler comes home from the hospital. The schedule now is for Houston to fly directly to Maine with Terry on the thirty-first. He spoke to the doctors and they've agreed to the timing."

"Good. January, are you absolutely positive that you want to—"

"Yes, Mother. My mind is made up."

"Oh, you do have your father's stubborn streak." She sighed again. "I won't mention your decision in the future. It would be like talking to the wall."

"Fine. Now we can discuss my wedding dress. And what you'll wear. And . .. oh, isn't this exciting? I'm getting married!"

Sara smiled. "Indeed, you are. All right, tell me what marvelous ideas you have for your dress. You don't have much time, you know. July thirty-first will be here in a flash."

"And I," January said dreamily, "will be Houston's January in July."

•   •   •

July 31

"Houston, slow down," Terry said. "I'm six-two, but I still can't cover the ground like you can."

"Sorry," Houston said, shortening his stride. "I appreciate your being my best man, Terry."

"So you've said six times. The honor is mine, as *I've* said six times. How much farther is it? I'm used to having a clear picture of things from the cockpit of a plane."

"January Hall is over the top of this rise." Houston quickened his step.

"There he goes again," Terry muttered. "Talk about an eager bridegroom." Houston had stopped, and Terry hurried to catch up with him. Terry whistled low and long. "Holy smokes, what a place. We're liable to get caught in the cross fire between the blue and the gray."

"It's something, isn't it?" Houston said, smiling.

"No joke."

"Well, let's go," Houston said. "This is my wedding day, man. It's also my birthday. It's January's birthday, too, did you know that?"

"A match made in heaven," Terry said.

"Yeah, well . . ." Houston began, then frowned.

"What's wrong?"

"You're a working man, Terry, just like I am. Maybe you can understand that January's money, her being a St. John, bothers me. We figured out the other problems, compromised, but there sure is a big one left. Cold, hard cash. I want to provide for my wife, give her a home, pay for the things she wants, but . . ."

"I hear what you're saying, Houston. But the St. Johns . . . I don't know, they're different. When Mr.

St. John was alive, he'd come right up in the cockpit and fly the plane for a while. When my wife . . . well, never mind."

"You're married?"

"I was. My wife died eight years ago. Mr. St. John heard that she was sick. He made arrangements for me to take her to the finest specialists in the country, flying her there in the company plane. In the end it didn't help, but I never forgot what he did for me."

"I'm sorry about your wife," Houston said.

"Yeah, me, too, but it was a long time ago. The point I'm trying to make is that the St. Johns care about people. They help a lot of folks with their money. What would you do? Tell Miss St. John . . . January . . . that it's fine if she wants to donate a quarter of a million dollars to a charity but she'll have to buy her own clothes at K-Mart? I don't see how you can pick and choose as to when she can be wealthy."

"I'm already doing that in a way," Houston said. "I just flew in a private jet."

"Yep."

"Dammit, Terry, what am I going to do? I'm getting married today. I probably shouldn't be getting married today with a problem this big unsolved."

Terry smiled. "But you're going to marry her, anyway."

"Damn right," he said, grinning. "Man, oh, man, I love that woman."

"Then trust in that love, Houston. Oh, Lord, there's nothing finer than a poetic pilot."

"Trust in that love," Houston said thoughtfully.

"Come on, Tyler, your bride awaits. You're positive that she said we didn't need to bring our own suits?"

"That's what she said. I gave her our measurements, and she assured me that everything would be here."

"Not bad," Terry said. "I get a new suit out of the deal."

"Well, a bride has the right to have the kind of wedding she wants."

"Ho-ho, now he's an expert on brides," Terry said, laughing. "There's nothing more obnoxious than a man who's newly in love. He doesn't rest until he's fixed up all his buddies with someone. Leave me out of your future matchmaking schemes, Houston. I have a mistress—that airplane—and a love affair going with the wild blue yonder."

"Lord, you really are poetic."

"Yep," he said, appearing rather pleased with himself. "Combine that with my stunning, blond good looks and excellent physique, and I'm a helluva guy."

"Modest too," Houston said, cocking an eyebrow at him.

"Well, nobody's perfect. I'm close, though, very close."

The men laughed and started off again.

Terry *was* a handsome devil, Houston thought, and he had a laid-back way of accepting life. He wasn't bitter or hard over the death of his wife. A poetic pilot, that was Terry Russell. "Trust in that love," Terry had said. Trust in the love Houston shared with January? He did! He really did. But, dammit, love wasn't always enough. Sometimes a man had to step in and take charge to fix things the way they ought to be.

Right, Houston thought dryly. He hadn't fixed anything. January's money was still there taunting him, no answer to that dilemma had been found, and he'd run out of time. Today, on July thirty-first, his and January's birthday, Miss January St. John would become the wife of Mr. Houston Tyler.

No, Houston thought suddenly, that wasn't who they were. They were the mistress and master of January Hall.

"Get the lead out, Terry," Houston said, then took off running.

"Hey," Terry yelled, sprinting after him, "this is a decrepit thirty-five-year-old body you're dragging around."

"Come on, old man."

"I'm with you, kid."

As the two men barreled up to the front porch of January Hall, a man stepped out of the door and raised his hand in a halting gesture.

"Whoa, gents," the man said. "Hello, Terry. It's good to see you."

"Mr. St. John," Terry said, nodding. "This is Houston Tyler. Houston, this is Mr. Robert St. John, January's uncle."

"I've heard good things about you, Houston," Robert said, shaking his hand.

"Thank you, sir."

"Oh, hell, don't call me sir. You're family now. Okay, listen up. I have a very important assignment here, you see. I'm not to allow you to come in the front door."

"Why not?" Houston said.

Robert shrugged. "Who understands women on the day of a wedding? They keep shoving me out of the way. I finally got the title of official lookout. You two are to go around back, through the kitchen, and up the rear stairs to the first bedroom on the left."

"I love it," Terry said, whooping with laughter. "The groom has to go to the servants' entrance. I wonder if January will have 'obey' in the vows."

Robert laughed.

Houston glowered.

"Come on, Houston," Terry said, punching him on the arm, "you might as well get used to doing as you're told."

"That's good advice, my boy," Robert said pleasantly.

"Okay, okay," Houston said, throwing up his hands.

"I have one other special assignment," Robert said, smiling.

"Oh?" Houston said.

"A surprise for you, Houston," Robert said. "Ta-da," he said with a sweep of his arm toward the door. A man and woman stepped out onto the porch.

"Austin! Sam!" Houston said. "How did . . . what are you . . . oh, man!"

Austin flung herself into Houston's arms and hugged him tightly. A smiling Samuel managed to shake Houston's hand. Houston quickly introduced them to Terry.

"Austin, how did you get here?" Houston said, smiling down at her.

"It was our mother. Our mother, if you can believe that. She managed to reach us on our cruise by having the Coast Guard call ship-to-shore. She said it just wasn't right that none of your family would be with you on your wedding day. We left the ship in a little boat, caught a plane, and here we are."

"You interrupted your honeymoon?" Houston said.

"We wouldn't have missed this for anything," Samuel said. "Congratulations, Houston. We met your January. She's a lovely woman."

"I'm so happy for you," Austin said, hugging him again, "and for January too. Now go. It's getting late."

"Yeah, okay, I'm going," Houston said. "I still can't believe you're here. Thank you. Thank you both."

"We love you," Austin said. "Go."

Houston smiled, then hurried away with Terry. Austin sighed dreamily. Samuel patted his pockets.

"What are you doing?" Austin said.

"Making sure I have a handkerchief or two. I figure you'll cry through the entire ceremony."

"Of course I will," she said, slipping her arm through his. "It's the only way to enjoy a beautiful wedding."

Samuel laughed in loving delight.

The kitchen was a beehive of activity, with several women Houston had never seen before bustling around. Tantalizing aromas wafted through the air.

"I'm hungry," Houston said.

"Tough," Terry said. "Where are the rear stairs?"

"This way. I want to see January too."

"No," Terry said. "Go."

Houston clomped up the back stairs. "What time s it?"

"Just after one o'clock. This tying of the knot is scheduled for two. Hustle your buns, Tyler."

"I'm hungry!"

"Cripe," Terry mumbled. "A pouting bridegroom."

On the upper floor the two men entered the first bedroom on the left.

"Would you look at that?" Terry said. "Hey, Houston, take a gander at those suits."

Houston grinned. "I'll be damned. They're like Rhett Butler wore: Short jackets, tails. January has us decked out like old-fashioned Southern gentlemen. Well, let's go for it. I'll use this shower; you go across the hall. I hope we can figure out how to get into these things."

Just before two o'clock, Robert appeared to escort Houston and Terry downstairs. Robert was also dressed in a suit reminiscent of the South.

"Lord, we're gorgeous," Robert said. "Ready, gents?"

"Yep," Terry said.

"No," Houston said. "I mean, yes, certainly."

"Nervous, Houston?" Terry asked.

"Hell, no," he said, brushing past him.

"He's nervous," Terry told Robert.

Downstairs, Houston glanced into the living room and saw the multitude of large baskets holding a variety of bright, fragrant flowers. A minister was standing at the front of the room, and Sara St. John and another woman were chatting with him, along with Austin and Sam. Sara and the other woman wore long dresses in pastel colors that appeared like they were straight out of *Gone With the Wind*. A small organ was against the wall, and a man seated himself in front of it.

"Houston," Robert said, "come here. You're to stand

by the living room door so that you can see January come down the stairs. I'll meet her, bring her to you, then you walk down the aisle together. Got it?"

"Got it."

"Terry," Robert went on, "go up by the minister. Who has the ring?"

"Got it," Terry said, patting his pocket.

The man began to play "The Wedding March" on the organ.

"This is it," Robert said.

"Oh, Lord," Houston said.

"If you pass out, Houston," Terry said, "I'm not even going to try to catch you. You'll break my body if you land on me."

"Move," Robert whispered.

The men took their places.

Houston looked up to the top of the stairs, and his heart thundered in his chest.

January, his mind hummed. Oh, January.

She was dressed in a white, floor-length lace dress that was scooped to the edge of her shoulders and cut low over her breasts. A pink satin ribbon circled her waist, the streamers trailing to the floor in back. A wide-brimmed hat with a pink ribbon adorned her head, and she carried a bouquet of pink rosebuds and baby's breath.

To Houston it seemed as though she had stepped out of another era, was the essence of beauty of the days of Southern grace and elegance. She was, indeed, the mistress of January Hall. He felt a tightening in his throat as he gazed up at her, his heart nearly bursting with love.

January started slowly down the sweeping staircase, one hand resting lightly on the banister, her gaze riveted on Houston.

Oh, how splendid he looked, she thought dreamily. And oh, how she loved him. It was perfect, all of it. They were January and Houston of January Hall, of a long-ago time. But yet, they would walk together into the now, and the future. It was something old, something new. Images borrowed from another time. But nothing blue. No, she carried nothing blue to depict a mood that was gloomy or sad. This was their day, hers and Houston's; their birthdays, their wedding day, their forever day.

"Bless you," Robert said, kissing her on the cheek when she reached the bottom of the stairs. He tucked her hand around his arm and took her to where Houston stood. "Love her, Houston," he said quietly.

"Yes, sir," Houston said, his gaze never leaving January. She slipped her arm through his. "You're beautiful. I love you, January."

"And I love you, Houston," she said, her eyes misting with tears. "You're beautiful too."

"Go," Robert whispered, his own eyes unusually bright.

It was all a blur.

January assumed she must be saying what she was supposed to be saying, because the minister kept smiling at her. She heard the deep rumble of Houston's voice but couldn't make out his words.

"Houston," Terry finally whispered. "Here, take the ring, put it on her finger."

Houston blinked. "What?"

Terry shoved the ring into his hand, and somehow it ended up on January's slender finger. Sara St.

John gave a ring to January, who stared at it blankly.

"Put it on Houston's finger, January," the minister said, chuckling.

"Oh," she said, doing as instructed.

More words were spoken.

"You may kiss the bride," the minister finally said to Houston.

"Who?" Houston said. Terry jabbed him in the ribs with his elbow. "Got it."

Houston brushed his lips over January's, then smiled at her. "Are we married?"

"I think so."

"Friends," the minister said, "may I present Mr. and Mrs. Houston Tyler, the mistress and master of January Hall."

"We're married!" January said, smiling brightly. "We did it, Houston. Oh, how I love you."

"And I love you."

It was hugs and kisses and handshakes. It was family and friends asking the newlyweds if they remembered any of the ceremony, only to be told quite indignantly that of course they did. It was tears of happiness and wishes for a wonderful future life together. It was a festive mood and a buffet of delicious food that was consumed with relish.

"Hungry," Houston muttered, heaping his plate full.

"Being married hasn't affected your appetite," January said.

"Magnolia," he said, laughing, "I wouldn't touch that statement with a ten-foot pole."

January blushed the same color as the pretty pink sash on her dress.

As the first streaks of the summer sunset drifted across the sky, Robert announced it was time to catch the boat. January and Houston stood on the porch of January Hall and waved good-bye until the group had disappeared from view.

She turned and smiled up at Houston. "Hello, Master Tyler."

"Hello, Mistress Tyler," he said, pulling her into his arms. "January Tyler. Lord, that sounds great."

"I think so too. Did you and Terry mind dressing like Rhett Butler?"

"No way. We thought we were very dashing. The wedding was nice, January, really nice. It was perfect for January Hall too. Hell, the whole day was perfect. Seems only fair that I give you a perfect night in return."

"Well, yes, that does seem fair. I've missed you so much."

"I missed you too. My family sends their love to you. Man, I still can hardly believe that Austin and Sam got here. That was fantastic. January, let's go upstairs."

She smiled and took his hand.

In the master suite, January gasped in surprise. "Oh, Houston, the wedding quilt you bought . . . it's on the bed."

"I made arrangements with your mother to see that it got up here where it belonged. Wherever we go to live, we'll have that quilt on the bed. I'm sentimental, you know."

"It's a beautiful quilt. Thank you for doing this. Houston, I have something for you too." She walked to the dresser and opened a drawer, returning with a folded paper in her hand. "This is my wedding gift to you," she said, giving it to him.

Houston unfolded the paper and read it, a frown knitting together his brows. "January, this is a deed to this island and to January Hall, registered in my name."

She ran her tongue nervously over her lips. "Houston, this house, this island, is yours. It's a home where you can bring your bride, where we'll live, raise our children. January Hall won't be a resort, it will be our haven. I can work here; you can work on the mainland. We'll create our own world right here, not worry about anything beyond our front door."

"This," he said, glancing again at the paper, "is your answer to our problem regarding your money?"

"We have no problem, Houston. January Hall is yours. I'm living with you in the home you chose for us. You said that January Hall always felt like home to you. Well, now we're here, together."

"Dammit, January, you're playing games," he said, his voice rising. "You keep saying this is my home, but you bought it!"

"It's my wedding gift to you, just as the quilt is yours to me."

"Oh, hell," he said with a snort of disgust, "like there's really a comparison there."

"There is, because they were both given in love. Oh, Houston, let us have this chance. We can be so happy here. I just know it. We can go into New York for the theater and baseball games, but the rest of the time we'll just be two people in love, living our lives the way we want to. It's the answer we've been looking for, Houston. It is."

He spun around and walked across the room, stopping with his back to her. January watched him, hardly breathing, as her heart raced.

Oh, please, Houston, she begged silently. Please.

He turned and flung the paper on top of the quilt. When his eyes met hers, they were cold, and his jaw was set in a tight, hard line.

"No," he said, his voice ominously low. "Did you honestly think I'd toss away my pride by telling myself that wedding gifts don't count in the overall picture? Hey, today is my birthday. Where's my present? What's next? How about title to the plane Terry flies? Everyone knows how much I like that plane."

"Houston, don't," she said, a sob catching in her throat.

"Don't what? Don't have a shred of pride left? Don't face facts, reality, just live here in marital bliss like a kept man? The hell I will, lady. What happened, January? Were you scared to death that I'd show up today announcing I'd bought us a tacky box in a middle-class suburb? Did you think you'd beat me to the punch, that January Hall was so special to me that I'd sell out, chuck the very essence of who I am and accept something worth this much from you? Well, no soap. Lord, I can't believe this," he said, raking a hand through his hair.

"Houston, I gave you January Hall out of love," she said, tears spilling onto her cheeks, "not as part of a scheme to strip you of your pride. I thought it would be the answer we were seeking."

"Well, you thought wrong," he said, starting toward the door.

"Where are you going?"

"For a walk. Alone."

"Houston, this is our wedding night."

He yanked open the door and turned to look at her. "Sorry, Magnolia," he said, a bitter edge to his voice, "but I forgot to make reservations at this hotel." He left the room and slammed the door closed behind him.

"Oh, Houston," January whispered, pressing her fingertips to her lips. Her trembling legs refused to hold her, and she sank to her knees on the floor. "*Houston!*" she screamed.

Her anguished cry echoed through the room, then silence fell, broken only by the sound of January's sobs.

Nine

Darkness had fallen with a heavy curtain, and the twinkling stars had nudged their way through the inky blanket to cast a silvery luminescence over the island.

Houston walked, his long legs covering the ground with amazing speed, to which he paid no attention. Emotions tumbled and raged within him; emotions of anger, frustration, confusion, and the greatest pain and loneliness he had ever known.

Time lost meaning, and still he walked.

With a jerk of surprise he stopped as he heard the sound of gentle waves lapping against the shore. He had, he realized, walked all the way to the far side of the island. He went down a grassy slope to the sandy beach, then stood staring out over the water. The stars reflected off the calm surface as though it were a black mirror, a mirror bouncing back all his 'houghts and inner turmoil, giving no quarter, no inch of room for peace.

"Ah, January," he said, his voice raspy. "Ah, damn."

He shoved his hands into his pockets, only then registering the fact that he was still wearing his wedding suit, which gave him the image of a gentleman of the Old South.

Southern gentleman, he thought with disgust. Sure. Right. No gentleman, Southern born and bred, nor a Yankee, would leave his bride crying and alone on their wedding night.

How good was he, he wondered, at loving? Oh, not the physical side of love, but the emotional part; the understanding, caring, the accepting, the compromising? How good was he, really, at meeting his woman halfway, joining her in the middle ground, finding *their* place without a fence between them?

He was lousy at that part of loving, he told himself, because January was crying on their wedding night.

Houston's mind skittered to the past, seeing January riding in the rickety pickup truck, eating out of cheap pottery at the inn. He saw her face glowing with excitement as she watched the fireworks on the Fourth of July. He envisioned her look of awe when she'd first seen the handmade wedding quilt, then saw again the joy in her eyes when she'd found it on their bed.

A handmade quilt, Houston thought. January could buy a thousand quilts from any country in the world. Quilts made of the finest material and costing more than his truck was worth. But she hadn't wanted those quilts, he knew that. *He'd* bought her the one that held special meaning, the one that had caused her face to light up with happiness and love that very night.

Houston stiffened as thoughts slammed against his mind. The quilt, his mind repeated over and over. The quilt. He could have sold his truck, taken the money to buy her the best and fanciest quilt in the country, and it wouldn't have meant as much to her as the one he'd given her.

Given her in love.

Houston pulled his left hand from his pocket and stared at the wedding band on his finger, sparkling in the starlight.

He hadn't thought about the rings during the wedding ceremony, he realized. He bought January's while he'd been home in Chicago helping his mother cope with his father's accident. The fact that January had slipped a ring on his finger, too, had passed in the hazy blur of what had been taking place.

He ran his thumb over the heavy band, felt the weight, knew it was expensive and made of the purest gold. It cost, no doubt, ten times what he'd paid for the one he'd placed on her finger.

Did that, he asked himself, measure their love for each other? Did the cost of the rings have any bearing on what was in their hearts and souls? Hell, no! Those rings were an outward sign; visible, tangible evidence of their deepest feelings.

Those rings had been given in love.

"Trust in that love," Terry had said.

Trust in that love, Houston repeated to himself. Trust it enough to know it could bear the weight of his and January's different backgrounds and social standings, of their glaring differences in regard to financial worth. Trust and believe in that love to the extent that it would give them the courage to find their *own* place, create their *own* world, where nothing would matter but the two of them.

A place like January Hall.

"Dear God," Houston whispered, dragging his hand down his face. "Oh, dear God, what have I done?"

January had given him January Hall in love.

And he had rejected that love, along with her gift, as he'd stepped back beyond the fence between them, hiding behind his pride, his misplaced sense of manliness.

He'd left her alone to cry on their wedding night.

Oh, dear God, what had he done?

He had to go to her, Houston thought frantically, see her, touch and hold her, beg her forgiveness.

Houston glanced at his watch, his heart thundering. Where had the time gone? he thought in a near panic. It was a little after eleven o'clock. There was less than one hour left in July. July belonged to him and to January together; it was theirs. He couldn't, wouldn't, allow July to slip into oblivion, having been swept away by January's tears.

He turned from the quiet water and began to run. With all the strength he possessed, with his heart, mind, and soul screaming January's name, he ran, his feet pounding as rapidly as his pulse. Sweat beaded his brow and dripped down his back, and still he pressed on, his lungs begging for mercy.

Then, at last, January Hall came into view. Houston quickened his pace even more as he dashed around the side, across the porch, then burst in the front door. He closed the door and leaned against it, gasping for breath.

"Houston?"

His head jerked up, and he saw January still in

her wedding dress, standing halfway down the sweeping staircase.

"Houston, dear heaven, what happened to you?" January said, not moving. "Is something chasing you?"

"Time," he rasped, glancing at his watch. "Oh, Lord, there's only eighteen minutes left."

"What?"

"Wait," he said, raising his hand. He shrugged out of his sweat-soaked jacket, dropped it on the floor, then bent over and gripped his knees, filling his lungs with fresh, healing air. He straightened again and looked at his watch. "Sixteen minutes. Damn."

"Were you drinking out there?" January asked.

Houston went to the bottom of the steps and looked up at her. "No, I wasn't drinking, I was thinking. Clearly, for a change. January, please listen to me. There isn't much time left."

"Time left? I don't understand."

"In July. Our July. I can't let July disappear with you crying. I can't. Will you listen to me?"

"Yes, of course," she said, coming down several steps. "I want to talk to you too. I'm sorry about January Hall. I thought I was doing the best thing for us and—"

"No, no, stay there. If I take you in my arms, I won't be able to think."

"All right, Houston," she said quietly. She sat down on the steps and wrapped her arms around her knees, her gaze riveted on him.

"January," he started, his voice thick with emotion, "I've made terrible mistakes. Everything was so confusing. The differences in our worlds seemed so big, so overwhelming and powerful. I was searching frantically for answers, looking so hard that I couldn't see what was right in front of me."

"What was it?"

"You. You have the gift of acceptance. Wherever you are, wherever you go, you take what life offers you, and you cherish it. I've seen you mingle with the rich, wear elegant clothes as naturally as breathing. And I've seen you in a rustic inn savoring the flavor of clam chowder in a cheap, chipped bowl. I've watched you move through an apartment worth vast sums of money, then give ten times that amount to a needy charity. You've worn faded jeans and padded around barefoot while flying in a private jet."

January nodded but didn't speak.

"And you fell in love," Houston went on, "and married, a middle-class construction worker. I saw it all, and still I insisted that we faced enormous problems. I was wrong. *We* didn't face them, *I* did. With your beautiful gift of acceptance, you follow your heart, living each moment to the fullest, passing no judgment, weighing nothing of material value against the joy you find wherever you go."

"Oh, Houston," she said, her eyes brimming with tears.

"But me? I've struggled under the weight of my pride, made your friends pass tests for me, prove that they were as human and real as the people I know. I accepted the existence of the limousine and the plane because it suited my purpose, then rejected your apartment and January Hall because I gave way to my pride again. Lord, I don't know how you put up with me."

"I love you," she said, tears spilling onto her cheeks.

"I know," he said, his voice thick. "Tonight"—he drew a ragged breath—"tonight I gave you a gift of a handmade wedding quilt. Tonight you gave me January Hall. Both were given in love. But I weighed and measured them against each other. I destroyed their meaning, what they represented by placing material values on them. I didn't trust in our love enough, January, to see that each of those gifts was equal in meaning, in caring, in loving."

January made no attempt to stop the flow of tears that continued to stream down her face. Houston looked at his watch.

"Oh, Lord, four minutes. January, please, please forgive me. I'm guilty of so much; of being narrow-minded and prejudiced because I was entering a world I didn't know or understand. I'm guilty of keeping the fence between us when there was no reason for it to be there. I'm guilty of demanding that people pass tests for me, of not trusting in our love enough, of not receiving with dignity gifts given in love. I'm sorry. *So damn sorry.* But, January? Through it all, during my blundering, my confusion, my mistakes, I never stopped loving you. Please give me another chance. January, please, say something before our July is gone!"

January got to her feet, lifted her dress to her ankles, and ran down the stairs. Houston opened his arms, and she flung herself against his chest wrapping her arms around his neck. He staggered slightly, then held her tightly to him, her feet dangling above the floor.

She tilted her head back to look at him. "Houston," she said, her voice choked with tears, "I love you. I will always love you. I understand what you've been going through, I really do. I know a man's pride is a fragile, precious thing, and I never wanted to destroy yours. I was trying so hard to show you that as long as I was with you, nothing else mattered. I thought we would be so happy here at January Hall."

"We will be. We will. Do you forgive me?"

"There's nothing to forgive. It's all behind us now. The future is ours."

He set her on her feet and looked at his watch. "Thirty seconds. Our future begins right now, in July, just as it should. You"—he pulled her close again—"are my January in July, my love, my life, my wife. I love you more than I can ever say."

"And I love you. Happy birthday, Houston."

He cradled her face in his hands and gazed at her, tears shimmering in his eyes. "Happy birthday, Magnolia."

And then he kissed her.

For better, for worse, January thought dreamily, in sickness and in health, and oh, yes, for richer, for poorer, she would always love Houston Tyler, the master of January Hall.

Epilogue

July 31—one year later

Houston stood on the back porch of January Hall and watched January where she sat on the ground beneath a tree, playing with a kitten. She laughed, and the happy sound brought a smile to Houston's lips. He went down the steps and hurried toward her.

"Houston," January said, looking up in surprise. "You're home early."

"I decided that as owner of Tyler Construction Company I had the authority to knock off ahead of schedule. After all, it's not every day of the year that a man celebrates his first wedding anniversary along with his and his wife's birthdays."

"But we exchanged gifts at breakfast." She picked up the kitten and kissed it on the nose. "I adore my present."

"Did you name her?"

"Her name is Magnolia."

Houston chuckled and settled on the ground next to January, resting his back against the tree.

"Confess, Houston," January said, smiling at him, "you came home early to play with your present."

"Well, I have manuals to read, buttons to push. That is a first-class shortwave radio you gave me. I can call out, receive messages, all kinds of great stuff. All I have to do is figure out how to work it."

"Personally I'd rather play with Magnolia. Oh, she's so fluffy and cute."

Houston smiled as the kitten chased after a piece of yarn that January trailed across the grass.

One year, he mused. One beautiful year. Though it hardly seemed possible, he loved January even more with every passing day. He'd grown in that year, taken the final steps necessary to meet her truly halfway, in that precious middle ground they cherished and protected.

He knew, really knew, that the monetary value of their gifts to each other on that special day meant nothing. The kitten and the radio had been given in love, and that was all that mattered. The expression of pure joy on January's face when he'd given her the furry bundle that morning was priceless, had no way of having a price tag attached to it.

"Terry will be up on Friday," January said. "We'll fly back to New York early Saturday, all right? I have a lot to do."

"Like what?"

"I have to stop by St. John Enterprises for more files and turn in my reports on the requests for grants I've already reviewed. Then, after I see the doctor, I think I'll treat myself to a new dress for the theater that night. On Sunday we have tickets to the baseball game. Terry will fly us back and stay over for a few days. He wants to do some fishing."

"Fine. As long as I don't have to fish with him. I hate fishing. It's dull, boring . . ." Houston stiffened. "Hold it. Doctor? What doctor? Why are you seeing a doctor? January? Is something wrong? Are you sick? You don't look sick. Talk to me."

She laughed. "I can't talk to you. You're using up all the air."

"January!"

"Houston," she said, smiling at him warmly. "I'm going to the doctor to confirm what I am thoroughly convinced is true."

He swallowed heavily. "What? What is it?"

"A baby."

Houston nodded slowly. "A baby." He paused. "A baby?" he yelled.

"Oh, you scared Magnolia."

He gripped January by the shoulders and turned her toward him. "A baby? You really think so?"

"I really do."

"Oh, January. Oh, this is fantastic! A little baby, a daughter, a tiny copy of you."

"There *are* such things as boy babies."

"Well, sure, that's okay, fine, no problem. If it's a boy, I'll teach him great stuff, and Terry can take him fishing. We'll just have a girl the next time. January, this is really some birthday and anniversary gift you're giving me."

"This one is ours together, my darling. We created it with our love, right here at January Hall."

He pulled her close and kissed her deeply, not releasing her until their hearts were racing. January rested her head on his shoulder and watched Magnolia chase the ball of yarn.

"January," Houston said, breaking the contented silence, "how do you feel about traditions?"

"I adore traditions, you know that. And so do you, since you're admittedly a very sentimental man. Why?"

"Well, this baby is going to be a Tyler, and there is a tradition in the Tyler family."

"Oh, now wait just a minute. I have a feeling I know where this is heading. I refuse to name this child San Antonio or Corpus Christi."

Houston hooted with laughter. "Gotcha."

"You dud," she said, laughing. "You were kidding."

"I want to name her Julie, which will remind me of July every time I hear it."

"Oh, Houston, that's lovely."

He wove his fingers through her silky, dark curls. "Lord, I'm a lucky man. I've just spent the happiest year of my life, there's a child of our love on the way, and"—he kissed her on the temple—"I have my very own January in July."

THE EDITOR'S CORNER

We are preparing to light five huge candles on our LOVESWEPT birthday cake next month. And, because we are celebrating this special anniversary, I've asked to take back the writing of the "Editor's Corner" to make a lot of special announcements.

You have a gala month to look forward to with wonderful books both in the LOVESWEPT line and in the Bantam Books general list. The historical Delaney trilogy is coming and will go on sale at the same time the LOVESWEPTs do. Here's what you have to anticipate.

THE DELANEYS, THE UNTAMED YEARS

Historical splendor of post-Civil War America.
Unforgettable characters who founded the Delaney Dynasty
Spellbinding adventure ablaze with passion.

COPPER FIRE
By Fayrene Preston
Set in the Colorado Territory, 1873, **COPPER FIRE** tells the story of the tenderhearted spitfire Brianne Delaney, whose search for her kidnapped twin brother leads her into the arms of a rugged, ruthless man.

WILD SILVER
By Iris Johansen
From Imperial Russia to the Mississippi delta, 1874, **WILD SILVER** follows the exquisite half-Apache outcast, Silver Delaney, who is held captive on a riverboat by its mysterious owner, a young and irresistible, fallen Russian prince.

GOLDEN FLAMES
By Kay Hooper
Moving from New York to the New Mexico/Arizona border, 1870, **GOLDEN FLAMES** trails Falcon Delaney, the broodingly handsome loner who's spent years tracing a stolen cache of Union gold. But now he turns his skills to tracking the secrets of the bewitching woman who has stolen his soul.

And, going on sale April 20, 1988, as part of Bantam's Grand Slam promotion you will see copies everywhere of the breathtaking and spine-tingling . . . **BRAZEN VIRTUE** by Nora Roberts.

The steamy summer streets of Washington are no match for the phone lines of Fantasy, Inc., where every man's dreams come true. The "hotline" works perfectly for its anonymous clients and the teachers and housewives who moonlight as call girls . . . until a brilliant madman plugs in with twisted passion. Introducing GRACE McCABE, a gorgeous bestselling mystery writer determined to trap her sister's killer, and ED JACKSON, the handsome and tenacious cop you first met in **SACRED SINS.**

(continued)

We have more thrilling news for you. We're going to run a fabulous, fun contest throughout our Fifth Year called the "Hometown Hunk Contest." We will reissue six marvelous LOVESWEPT's (by six marvelous authors, of course) that were first published in the early days. The titles and authors are:

IN A CLASS BY ITSELF by Sandra Brown
FOR THE LOVE OF SAMI by Fayrene Preston
C.J.'S FATE by Kay Hooper
THE LADY AND THE UNICORN by Iris Johansen
CHARADE by Joan Elliot Pickart
DARLING OBSTACLES by Barbara Boswell

In the backs of our June, July, and August LOVESWEPTs we will publish "cover notes" just like those we use here at Bantam to create covers. These notes will describe the heroine and hero, give a teaser on the plot, and suggest a scene from the book for the cover. Your part in the contest will be to see if a great looking man in your own hometown fits our description and your ideas about what the hero of one of these books looks like. If so, you enter him in the contest (contest blanks will be in the books starting month-after-next, too), along with his picture. The "hometown hunk" who is selected will be the model for a new cover of the book! We hope you'll find absolutely great looking men who are just perfect for the covers of these six great LOVESWEPTs. We can't wait to start judging those pictures! Indeed, a dozen women in the company who've heard about the contest are just begging to help open the mail!

And now for our terrific romances next month!

She started it all with LOVESWEPT #1, **HEAVEN'S PRICE**— Sandra Brown. And, naturally, we asked Sandra to lead off our Fifth Birthday list. Now you can relish **ADAM'S FALL**, LOVE-SWEPT #252, the thrilling story that brings back two great characters from **FANTA C.** Heroine Lilah Mason is challenged like she's never been before when she encounters ADAM CAV-ANAUGH again. Adam's down, but not out, flat on his back— yet he and Lilah learn he can still fall!

And, now it is a great pleasure to introduce two talented writers making their debuts with LOVESWEPT.

First, we have Tami Hoag presenting us with **THE TROUBLE WITH J.J.**, LOVESWEPT #253. Here's all the humor and heart-warming romance of two great people—lovely Genna Hastings and devastating J.J. Hennessy. She's the adorable lady next door; he's her new neighbor with rippling muscles and mile-wide shoulders. A don't miss read, for sure!

Next, there's **THE GRAND FINALE**, LOVESWEPT #254, by Janet Evanovich. **THE GRAND FINALE** is riotously funny and in the opening chapter pizza tycoon Berry Knudsen literally falls for tall, dark, muscular Jake Sawyer. She didn't really mean to, but somehow she got a perfect view of the perfect man through
(continued)

his bedroom window! Jake doesn't have her arrested for peeping because he's having too much fun watching her squirm as she tries to explain herself!

HOLD ON TIGHT, LOVESWEPT #255, is Deborah Smith's second book for us. You'll remember that her first was a wonderful island fantasy. **HOLD ON TIGHT,** a very different but equally strong love story, shows Deborah's range. It's set in both a small Southern town, and the big city of Birmingham and features sophisticated Dinah Sheridan, a former beauty queen turned politician wooed by Rucker McClure, an irreverent best-selling journalist/author. As Deborah says "the teasing, provocative Rucker McClure is just about as sexy as a man can get!" We're sure that you won't want to let go of **HOLD ON TIGHT.**

Josh Long's men—and his lovely wife, Raven—are back to help out one of Kay Hooper's most devastatingly sexy heroes ever in **OUTLAW DEREK,** LOVESWEPT #256. A beguiling and beautiful woman wanders into the life of a longtime loner and sets him on fire with love. In the midst of danger, Derek Ross gentles the sweet spirit of Shannon Brown in one of Kay's most memorable and touching romances ever.

And last, but never, never least is our own Iris Johansen, who will return next August to celebrate *her* fifth anniversary as a published author. Iris has created for us a very special birthday present, **MAN FROM HALF MOON BAY,** LOVESWEPT #257. Surprise. Panic. Then desire like an electric shock filled Sara O'Rourke when she saw Jordan Bandor across the crowded room. For eighteen months she'd lived free of the man from the harsh, unforgiving Australian outback who'd swept her off her feet, then wrapped her in a seductive web of sensual pleasure that left no room for work or friends. And now these two passionate people must work out their relationship in an atmosphere of desperate danger!

We started LOVESWEPT in a marketplace full of romances. Some said we'd never last. But we've been here for five happy years because of *your* support. Thank you from the bottom of our hearts, and here's to five more wonderful years!

Carolyn Nichols

Carolyn Nichols
    Editor

LOVESWEPT
Bantam Books
666 Fifth Avenue
New York, NY 10103

The first Delaney trilogy

Heirs to a great dynasty, the Delaney brothers were united by blood, united by devotion to their rugged land . . . and known far and wide as

THE SHAMROCK TRINITY

Bantam's bestselling LOVESWEPT romance line built its reputation on quality and innovation. Now, a remarkable and unique event in romance publishing comes from the same source: THE SHAMROCK TRINITY, three daringly original novels written by three of the most successful women's romance writers today. Kay Hooper, Iris Johansen, and Fayrene Preston have created a trio of books that are dynamite love stories bursting with strong, fascinating male and female characters, deeply sensual love scenes, the humor for which LOVESWEPT is famous, and a deliciously fresh approach to romance writing.

THE SHAMROCK TRINITY—Burke, York, and Rafe: Powerful men . . . rakes and charmers . . . they needed only love to make their lives complete.

☐ *RAFE, THE MAVERICK by Kay Hooper*

Rafe Delaney was a heartbreaker whose ebony eyes held laughing devils and whose lilting voice could charm any lady—or any horse—until a stallion named Diablo left him in the dust. It took Maggie O'Riley to work her magic on the impossible horse . . . and on his bold owner. Maggie's grace and strength made Rafe yearn to share the raw beauty of his land with her, to teach her the exquisite pleasure of yielding to the heat inside her. Maggie was stirred by Rafe's passion, but would his reputation and her ambition keep their kindred spirits apart?   (21846 • $2.75)

LOVESWEPT

☐ *YORK, THE RENEGADE* by *Iris Johansen*

Some men were made to fight dragons, Sierra Smith thought when she first met York Delaney. The rebel brother had roamed the world for years before calling the rough mining town of Hell's Bluff home. Now, the spirited young woman who'd penetrated this renegade's paradise had awakened a savage and tender possessiveness in York: something he never expected to find in himself. Sierra had known loneliness and isolation too—enough to realize that York's restlessness had only to do with finding a place to belong. Could she convince him that love was such a place, that the refuge he'd always sought was in her arms?

(21847 • $2.75)

☐ *BURKE, THE KINGPIN* by *Fayrene Preston*

Cara Winston appeared as a fantasy, racing on horseback to catch the day's last light—her silver hair glistening, her dress the color of the Arizona sunset . . . and Burke Delaney wanted her. She was on his horse, on his land: she would have to belong to him too. But Cara was quicksilver, impossible to hold, a wild creature whose scent was midnight flowers and sweet grass. Burke had always taken what he wanted, by willing it or fighting for it; Cara cherished her freedom and refused to believe his love would last. Could he make her see he'd captured her to have and hold forever?

(21848 • $2.75)

Bantam Books, Dept. SW4, 414 East Golf Road, Des Plaines, IL 60016

Please send me the books I have checked above. I am enclosing $_____ (please add $1.50 to cover postage and handling). Send check or money order—no cash or C.O.D.s please.

Mr/Ms _____

Address _____

City/State _____ Zip _____

SW4—2/88

Please allow four to six weeks for delivery. This offer expires 8/88.
Prices and availability subject to change without notice.